YOU'LL CHEER ALL OVER AGAIN FOR . . .

THE SAN FRANCISCO 49ERS—pro football's Team of the Eighties and winners of four Super Bowl Championships. Led by their great all-pro quarterback, Joe Montana, the Niners dominated the decade and capped it off with their biggest Super Bowl win of all following the 1989 season.

WAYNE GRETZKY—the hockey superstar who was a pro at fifteen and a record breaker for the entire decade. Early in the 1989–90 season, the amazing Gretzky, not yet twenty-nine, became the leading scorer in NHL history, and is now often dubbed "the single greatest hockey player to ever lace on a pair of skates."

THE 1988 DODGERS—the "miracle" team that won the first game of the World Series in one of the most dramatic comebacks in Series history, then went on to become world champions in five games, defeating the powerful Oakland A's—after everyone said it couldn't be done!

MICHAEL JORDAN—portrait of the National Basketball Association's airborne scoring champion. The superstar guard of the Chicago Bulls can do it all on the court and is widely considered the game's most exciting player as the sport enters the 1990s.

All your favorites are here, up-close and personal, in the book that will keep you on the edge of your seat to the very last page.

Books by Bill Gutman

Sports Illustrated/BASEBALL'S RECORD BREAKERS
Sports Illustrated/GREAT MOMENTS IN BASEBALL
Sports Illustrated/GREAT MOMENTS IN PRO FOOTBALL
Sports Illustrated/PRO FOOTBALL'S RECORD BREAKERS
Sports Illustrated/STRANGE AND AMAZING BASEBALL
  STORIES
Sports Illustrated/STRANGE AND AMAZING FOOTBALL
  STORIES
BASEBALL'S HOT NEW STARS
GREAT SPORTS UPSETS
PRO SPORTS CHAMPIONS
STRANGE AND AMAZING WRESTLING STORIES

Available from ARCHWAY Paperbacks

PRO SPORTS CHAMPIONS

BILL GUTMAN

AN ARCHWAY PAPERBACK
Published by POCKET BOOKS

New York   London   Toronto   Sydney   Tokyo   Singapore

AN ARCHWAY PAPERBACK *Original*

An Archway Paperback published by
POCKET BOOKS, a division of Simon & Schuster Inc.
1230 Avenue of the Americas, New York, NY 10020

ISBN: 0-671-69334-4

First Archway Paperback printing October 1990

10 9 8 7 6 5 4 3 2 1

To my uncle and aunt,
John and Madeline Tausek,
with continued gratitude

Contents

1

THE SAN FRANCISCO 49ERS
Team of the Eighties

In 1988 the San Francisco 49ers joined some very select gridiron company. A year later they took another step upward and are now considered one of the greatest football teams of all time.

There have been many fine professional football teams over the years, memorable ball clubs with great individual stars. Although football has not produced a dynasty to equal the New York Yankees in baseball or the Boston Celtics in basketball, there have been a number of teams that have remained at or near the top for a long period of time.

For instance, the 1950s witnessed a number of fine football teams, such as the Los Angeles Rams, the New York Giants, and the Baltimore Colts. But the Team of the Fifties had to be the Cleveland Browns. They were coached by the innovative Paul Brown, quarterbacked by the resourceful Otto Graham, and in the last half of the decade featured the running of the incomparable Jim Brown. The Browns won the National Football League title three times

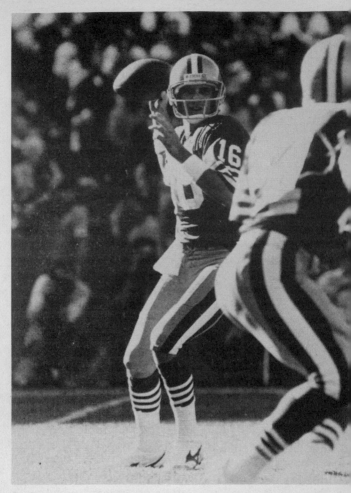

Joe Montana is football's all-time, top-rated quarterback and has been outstanding in each of the 49ers' four Super Bowl victories. In fact, many now call him the best ever at his position. (Courtesy San Francisco 49ers)

and appeared in the championship game on seven occasions.

By 1960 there was a new powerhouse on the horizon. After losing the NFL title game to Philadelphia in 1960, the Green Bay Packers dominated pro football for the remainder of the decade. Coached by the dynamic Vince Lombardi, the Packers won five NFL titles and the first two Super Bowls ever played. Many members of that team are now in the Pro Football Hall of Fame. Without a doubt, the Packers were the Team of the Sixties.

Then in the 1970s another team made football history by winning the Super Bowl a record four times. They were the Pittsburgh Steelers, coached by Chuck Noll and featuring Terry Bradshaw, Franco Harris, "Mean" Joe Greene, Jack Lambert, Jack Ham, Lynn Swann, and Mel Blount. Those were just a few of the individual stars who helped make the Steelers a great ballclub, surely the Team of the Seventies.

At the outset of the 1980s there was little indication as to which, if any, team would emerge as the Team of the Eighties. But by the time another ten-year period drew to a close, there was no question about which franchise would be remembered in the same way the Browns, Packers, and Steelers had been. The San Francisco 49ers tied the Steelers' record of winning four Super Bowl championships in a single decade.

The Niners became NFL World Champions in 1981, 1984, and again in 1988. Then in 1989 the team from the City by the Bay won number four by dominating the playoffs as no club before them had, trouncing the Denver Broncos, 55–10, in a record-setting Super Bowl performance that will be talked about for years.

San Francisco has maintained its high level of excellence during the decade despite personnel changes

3

and challenges from a number of very good football teams. But it didn't happen overnight. Though the Niners had some strong teams in the early 1970s, they quickly fell back, reaching the .500 mark only once after 1972.

By 1978 the club had hit rock bottom with a 2–14 record and had gone through five head coaches in four years. It seemed there was no game plan for rebuilding the ballclub. But, in reality, there was. It started in 1977, when Edward J. DeBartolo, Jr. became the team's owner. He began organizing slowly and carefully. In January of 1979 he hired Bill Walsh as his new coach and general manager. The change began.

Walsh came to the Niners with nearly twenty years of college and pro coaching experience, as well as having a reputation as a creative coach who worked especially well with quarterbacks and receivers. When he took over the team in 1979 he found a rookie quarterback out of Notre Dame waiting for him. His name was Joe Montana. Montana didn't have the greatest arm in the world and he wasn't as big or strong as some other quarterbacks. Nor was he lightning fast out of the pocket. But at Notre Dame they called him the Comeback Kid because, above all, Joe Montana knew how to win. To many Irish rooters it seemed as if he pulled games out in the fourth quarter like a magician pulls rabbits from a hat.

But despite the arrival of Montana and the other changes, the Niners didn't look like much in 1979, Walsh's first season at the helm. In fact, the club had its second straight 2–14 season, the same year the Pittsburgh Steelers closed out their Team of the Seventies decade by winning their fourth Super Bowl.

As for Montana, he was a backup to Steve DeBerg

4

and got to throw just 23 passes that year. Yet in one season the ballclub had gone from almost last in the NFL in total offense to first in passing and sixth overall. So Coach Walsh was beginning to work his magic. The next year the club improved to 6–10, and once again the offense shined. In the second half of that season, Coach Walsh made another move that would affect the club's fortunes the rest of the decade.

He decided to make a commitment to Joe Montana as the team's quarterback. Montana started seven of the team's final ten games, including the last four. Though he was in there just long enough to throw 273 passes, he nevertheless led the NFL and set a 49ers record with a 64.5 completion percentage. Along the way, he threw for 15 touchdowns and had only nine interceptions. In addition, he was an especially cool and effective quarterback in clutch situations. Coach Walsh described his quarterback's talents:

"People who say Joe only has an average arm are mistaken," he said. "Because his delivery is not a flick of the wrist like Terry Bradshaw's, they think it's not strong. But Joe can throw on the run while avoiding a pass rush. He doesn't have to be totally set. He is not a moving platform like some others who are mechanical and can only do well when everything is just right. Joe performs just as well under stress."

Montana would soon make his coach look like a prophet. Yet despite the team's overall improvement, no one was really prepared for what was about to happen in 1981. The club continued to rebuild with five rookies, five new players from trades, and ten free agents. When three of the rookies—Ronnie Lott, Carlton Williamson, and Eric Wright—earned starting berths in the defensive secondary, critics said the Niners would be in trouble because of their inexperience.

But there was balance. Defensive end Fred Dean and middle linebacker Jack "Hacksaw" Reynolds were both veterans who could still play the game. In the space of a single year, the defense had made great strides, along with the ever-improving offense. By midseason the team was in the thick of the race with a 6–2 record, and they did even better in the second half, winning seven of their final eight games. The result was a sensational 13–3 record and first place in the NFC West.

It was one of the biggest turnarounds in NFL history. In addition, Joe Montana justified Coach Walsh's faith in him by leading the NFC in passing. Montana, receiver Dwight Clark, center Randy Cross, defensive end Fred Dean, safety Dwight Hicks, and rookie Ronnie Lott would all make it to the Pro Bowl. But now the question was how the untested Niners would do in the playoffs.

They looked good in their first game, beating the New York Giants, 38–24. That hurdle cleared, the team now had to go up against the always-tough Dallas Cowboys for the NFC championship. The winner would be headed for the Super Bowl. In the eyes of many, this was the game where Joe Montana began to achieve greatness and the Niners began emerging as the Team of the Eighties.

Montana wasn't having one of his better days in this seesaw battle. Dallas had a 17–14 lead at the half. In the third quarter the Niners took the lead back at 21–17. But a Cowboys' field goal made it 21–20, and then a fumble recovery by Dallas led to the go-ahead score, making it 27–21 in the fourth period. When the Niners got the ball again, Montana threw an intercep-

All-Pro safety Ronnie Lott is the 49ers' leader on defense and has been an important part of their Super Bowl–winning formula. (Courtesy San Francisco 49ers)

tion. It didn't look good. Then with 4:54 remaining, San Francisco took over once again, this time at their own 11-yard line.

Montana began leading his team on a long drive, mixing his running and pass plays to perfection. It finally came down to one big play. The Niners had a third-down play with the ball at the Dallas six. There were 58 seconds left.

At the snap, Montana dropped back to pass. He looked for Freddie Solomon on the left side of the end zone, but the little wideout was covered. Joe then ran to his right. Even with 6'9" Ed "Too Tall" Jones right in front of him, he lofted a pass toward the back of the end zone, where Dwight Clark made a leaping catch for the go-ahead score. The clutch play—still remembered today as "The Throw and The Catch" —put the game away, 28–27, and the Niners were off to the Super Bowl.

In the big one they met the Cincinnati Bengals, another turnaround team, which had gone from 6–10 to 12–4 in the AFC Central. The Bengals' quarterback was Ken Anderson, whom Bill Walsh was also cred-ited with developing when he was an assistant at Cincy. The two teams had met in the regular season, and the Niners had taken a 21–3 victory, helping to make them the favorites.

The 49ers didn't disappoint in the first half. With Montana leading the way, San Francisco forged to a 20–0 halftime lead, and the game seemed all but over. But the Bengals fought back after intermission. They scored twice to make it 20–14, and the outcome was suddenly up for grabs.

In the final session, the Niners played ball control as another pair of Ray Wersching field goals upped the lead to 26–14. Though a last-minute Bengals touchdown brought the final score to 26–21, the Niners had done it. They had gone from a 6–10 team in 1980 to Super Bowl champions in one season. To do that, the club had won 16 of 19 games, including the playoffs.

In the Super Bowl, Joe Montana had thrown sparingly, but he completed 14 of 22 passes for 157 yards and a score. For his efforts, he was named the game's Most Valuable Player. Once again Coach Walsh praised his young quarterback.

"Joe Montana will be the great quarterback of the future," the coach said. "He is one of the coolest competitors of all time, and he has just started."

The next logical question was one always asked of sports champions. Could they repeat? The Niners thought so. But 1982 wasn't their year. A players' strike shortened the season to nine games, and the team couldn't seem to win at home. They finished at 3–6 and were out of the playoffs despite the fact that Montana and Dwight Clark each had a tremendous year. Several other individuals had Pro Bowl seasons, but the magic of the year before was clearly gone.

That was why the 1983 season was a pivotal one. The team kept adding personnel, trying to shore up their weak spots. One major change came at running back. Speedy Wendell Tyler came over from the Rams to play halfback, and the fullback was a rookie out of Nebraska named Roger Craig. With Montana, Clark, Solomon, and the tough defense doing their job again, the Niners regained the NFC West championship with a 10–6 record. But this time they were edged out by the Washington Redskins, 24–21, in the NFC championship game. There would be no return to the Super Bowl, but at least the ballclub had reestablished itself as one of the league's best.

Then in 1984 the Niners put it all together again. In

fact, they dominated the entire season as few teams ever have, getting stronger and stronger as the season continued. There were some close ones at the beginning, some blowouts near the end. When it was over, the Niners had compiled an incredible, 15–1 regular season record, their only loss being a 20–17 defeat at the hands of the Steelers.

The club had scored 475 points on offense, a team record, while the defense allowed just 227 points, the lowest total in the entire NFL. And there were some great individual performances as well, with ten starters picked to play in the Pro Bowl.

Joe Montana again led the way, firmly establishing himself as perhaps the premier quarterback in all of football. He threw for 3,630 yards while completing 64.5 percent of his passes. Included were 28 touchdowns as opposed to ten interceptions, and his quarterback rating was a spectacular 102.9, by far the best in the league.

The NFC playoff game was relatively easy for the Niners. Montana threw for a pair of first-quarter touchdowns against the New York Giants, and from there the defense did its job. San Francisco won, 21–10. Then in the NFC championship game, the defense was even better, shutting out the Chicago Bears, 23–0, clinching a second trip to the Super Bowl.

But this one wouldn't be easy. The Niners' opponents were the Miami Dolphins, a 14–2 team over the regular season. Coach Don Schula's ballclub was not only deep and balanced, but boasted second-year quarterback Dan Marino, who had just finished rewriting the NFL record book. Marino threw for more than 5,000 yards, with 48 touchdowns, and was seen as a challenge to Montana for the title of best in the league.

So the game was billed as a shootout between Montana and Marino.

But like many shootouts, it turned out to be one-sided. The opening quarter was competitive. The Dolphins scored first on a field goal, but Montana drove the Niners right back and hit reserve running back Carl Monroe with a 33-yard scoring aerial. Then it was Marino's turn. He moved the Dolphins 70 yards and capped it with a two-yard scoring toss. The kick made it a 10–7 game at the end of one period. As former coach turned sportscaster John Madden noted, it was up to the Niner defense to pressure Marino.

"Never let him get comfortable back there," Madden said. "If you do, he'll kill you."

The defense began applying the pressure in the second period. All the Dolphins could manage was a pair of field goals, while Montana and his offense went to work. One drive ended with an eight-yard scoring pass to Roger Craig. Another was finished when Montana himself ran it over from the six. And a third resulted in a two-yard score by Craig. At the half it was 28–16, the Niners firmly in charge.

That's the way it remained. The San Francisco defense harassed Marino and his receivers all over the field, while Montana coolly directed the offense. When the smoke cleared, San Francisco had its second world title, a surprisingly easy 38–16 victory. And along the way Joe Montana carved yet another notch in his gun, winning the MVP prize by connecting on 24 of 35 passes for 331 yards and three scores. He also ran for another 59 yards. It was truly a great performance.

But with five more seasons remaining in the decade, the question of Team of the Eighties was still unanswered. Though the Niners remained winners

Versatile Roger Craig once gained over 1,000 yards rushing and 1,000 yards receiving in the same season. The star running back helped make the 49ers the Team of the Eighties. (Courtesy San Francisco 49ers)

and playoff bound each year, 1985 turned out to be the year of the Chicago Bears, and 1986 was dominated by the New York Giants. The Niners were 10–6 and 10–5–1 during those two seasons. Roger Craig became an All-Pro as a running back, and a young wide receiver from Mississippi Valley State, Jerry Rice, was quickly becoming the league's most dangerous deep threat.

In 1985 the high-stepping Craig became the first back to gain more than 1,000 yards rushing and 1,000 yards receiving in the same season. In 1986 Rice exploded for 1,570 yards on 86 catches in just his second year. The constant was still Joe Montana, with lifetime stats that already made him the top-rated passer of all time. He had even bounced back from major back surgery in 1986 to play again before the season ended.

So when the Niners finished with a 13–2 record in 1987—including three replacement games because of another players' strike—they once again appeared to be the best team in football. Rice set a new NFL record by catching 22 touchdown passes in just 12 games, while Montana threw a career high of 31 touchdowns, giving him a league-leading quarterback rating of 102.1. Yet in the NFC playoff game against Minnesota, the club unexpectedly came up short, the Vikes executing to near perfection on offense and winning a 36–24 decision.

That was why 1988 loomed as all important. Despite heroics from the usual cast of characters, the team was a bit spotty in the regular season. But they finished strong, compiling a 10–6 record and winning the NFC West title for a third straight year. Along the way, Craig set a team record with 1,502 yards rushing, while Rice caught 64 passes for 1,306 yards. But the thing all the Niners wanted was a third Super Bowl triumph.

Maybe it was the desire to prove they belonged with the old Browns, Packers, and Steelers that drove them. The team started the playoffs with a 34–9 win, beating Minnesota, then shellacked the Bears, 28–3, in the NFC championship game. That earned them a trip to Miami for Super Bowl XXIII, where they would once again be meeting the Cincinnati Bengals, a team that had rebounded from a 4–11 record in 1987 to a 12–4 mark in 1988. The game turned out to be a struggle.

Despite the presence of Montana and his offense, the first half was a defensive stalemate, the teams trading field goals and going into their locker rooms tied at 3–3. So with 30 minutes of football remaining, the game was up for grabs. It was the Bengals who made the first move to take it.

Jim Breech connected on a 43-yard field goal early in the third period, to make it 6–3. Then Mike Cofer tied it for the Niners late in the session, hitting from 32 yards out. On the ensuing kickoff, Cincinnati's Stanford Jennings ran the ball up the middle, burst through the Niner coverage and sprinted 93 yards for a touchdown. Breech's extra point made it a 13–6 game after three periods. To win, San Francisco would have to come from behind once again.

Montana began his comeback magic. He used his two best weapons, Craig and Rice, to bring his club back. On the Niners' next possession, the Comeback Kid hit Rice for a 31-yard gain, then Craig for 40 more, and finally Rice from the 14 for the score. Cofer's kick tied it at 13–13. The two teams then battled without any more scoring until Breech connected from 40 yards out with a little over three minutes left. It was 16–13, and the Niners might only have one more chance.

When San Francisco could only bring the kickoff out to the eight-yard line, the Bengals rejoiced. San Francisco was 92 yards away with just three minutes left. But when one of the Bengals said to veteran receiver Cris Collinsworth, "We got 'em now," Collinsworth shot back without hesitation:

"Have you taken a look at who's quarterbacking? He's not human."

Sure enough, Montana began driving the Niners up the field. A short pass to Craig netted eight yards, then a quickie to tight end John Frank got seven more and a first down. Rice caught one for seven before Craig was stopped after one. That gave them a third and two at the 31. But Craig then ran for four and another first down. There was now 1:54 left.

After a timeout Montana went back to work. He hit Rice for 17 yards, then Craig for 13. The ball was now at the Bengals' 35 with 1:22 remaining. After a ten-yard penalty, Montana threw to Rice on a deep slant-in, good for 27 yards and a first down on the 18. An eight-yard completion to Craig put the ball at the ten with 39 seconds left. On the next play Montana calmly faked to Rice and went to his other wide receiver, John Taylor, who caught the ball for a ten-yard score, perhaps the biggest score in the history of the franchise. The kick made it 20–16, and that was the way it ended.

The 49ers were champions once more, with Rice winning the MVP on the strength of 11 catches for 215 yards. Montana had another great game, with 23 of 36 for 357 yards and two scores. What's more, he had passed his team to victory in the closing minutes of a hard-fought game. His latest heroics had come in the Super Bowl, and his magic touch enabled his team to win the championship for the third time in eight years.

Record-setting Jerry Rice of the 49ers is considered the most explosive wide receiver in all of pro football. The bigger the game, the better he seems to play. (Courtesy San Francisco 49ers)

As the decade of the 1980s drew to a close, the 49ers seemed to be growing stronger, even with head coach Bill Walsh's retirement following the 1988 season. He was replaced by former defensive coordinator George Seifert. Joe Montana and the troops put together another great year in 1989, winning the NFC West with a 14–2 record. In fact the offense now had more weapons than ever. For several years the attack had centered around Montana, Craig, and Rice. But John Taylor had emerged as close to the equal of Rice at the other wide receiver spot, and fullback Tom Rathman produced at near All-Pro level, blocking like a demon and catching more than 70 passes.

All Joe Montana did was put together one of the greatest seasons any quarterback ever had. Mr. Cool completed 70.2 percent of his passes, threw for 26 TDs against just eight interceptions, and had a career-high quarterback rating of 112.4, best by far in the entire league. And in the playoffs the entire team caught fire. First the Niners drubbed the tough Minnesota Vikings, 41–13. From there they took the NFC title by whipping the Rams, 30–3. Then was back to the Super Bowl against the Denver Broncos.

Denver never had a chance. While the Niner defense stopped quarterback John Elway and the Bronco offense, Montana and company set records. Joe threw for five touchdown passes, three of them to Jerry Rice, and the Niners blew out the Broncos by a Super Bowl record score, 55–10. Montana completed 22 of 29 passes for 297 yards, and was the Most Valuable Player for the third time. The Team of the Eighties had been officially crowned.

More than ever, the 49ers found themselves compared to the great teams of the past—the Browns,

Packers, and Steelers. But as All-Pro safety Ronnie Lott said after the slaughter of the Broncos, "Now I'd like to match us up with any of those other Super Bowl teams."

Many agreed. The Niners were being called one of the greatest teams of all time, and Joe Montana was hailed as perhaps the best ever at his position. The most frightening news for the other 27 NFL teams entering the decade of the nineties is this: the San Francisco 49ers may not be finished yet. Their goal is to become the first team ever to win three straight Super Bowls. It would be tough to bet against them.

2

SUGAR RAY ROBINSON
The One and Only

His real name was Walker Smith, an ordinary name of no real distinction. Had he not changed it, however, the name of Walker Smith would be known to boxing fans the world over. But because he was still underage when he began boxing, Walker Smith had to use another name. That name was Ray Robinson, and when a sportswriter saw how skilled he was in the ring, he commented that the youngster was "as sweet as sugar."

From that time on it was always "Sugar" Ray Robinson, the original "Sugar Ray" and the man most universally acknowledged as the greatest fighter ever. Performing in a totally different era, an era in which fighters went into the ring on a regular basis, Sugar Ray Robinson had 202 fights, winning 175 and losing just 19. He had six draws and two no contests. All that took place after an amateur career of 160 bouts.

Yet even his fine pro career is deceiving. For Sugar Ray fought until he was nearly forty-five years old. That was when most of his losses came, and against fighters who wouldn't have climbed into the ring with him years earlier. At one point, closer to the beginning of his career, the Sugar man had a record of 119–1–2. At the outset of his career he fought for prestige and artistry; later in his career it was strictly for money. There were no multimillion-dollar paydays then as there are now.

In going up against all the great fighters of the day—some of them, three, four, and five times—Sugar Ray won the welterweight title, then the middleweight title. In fact, he set a boxing record by winning the middleweight crown on five separate occasions. He even went after the light heavyweight title and was easily outpointing a good fighter named Joey Maxim when he collapsed from dehydration and heat exhaustion. The fight was outdoors in a temperature that exceeded 100 degrees. That was the only time Sugar Ray Robinson didn't finish a fight.

Sugar Ray was to boxing what Jim Brown was to football, Mickey Mantle to baseball, or Magic Johnson to basketball. He combined speed and power and had the ability to do what both quick little men and big powerful men could do. In other words, he was extremely fast with both his hands and feet, an artist who could box rings around most opponents. But he could also hit, with the power to take a man out with either hand. It was that power that caused 110 of his fights to end by knockout.

Maybe it was the great light-heavyweight champion Archie Moore who best summed up the essence of Ray Robinson. Said ageless Archie, "I don't know anybody better at his craft than he was. He was a stylist. He never copied anything off anybody. But generations of fighters have copied his style, including [Muhammad] Ali."

No fighter wanted to look across the ring and see Sugar Ray Robinson ready to come at him. Even today, most boxing experts consider Robinson to be, pound for pound, the best ever. (AP/Wide World Photos)

Perhaps the most well known and exciting fighter of the late 1970s and the 1980s, Sugar Ray Leonard, admittedly took the name of the master and is proud he can keep it alive. But as great a fighter as Leonard has been, most experts say that not even he has the consummate skills of Sugar Ray Robinson.

Though some sources list his birth year as 1920, *Ring Magazine,* long considered the official bible of boxing, says that Walker Smith, Jr. was born in Detroit, Michigan, on May 3, 1921. He was a street kid to whom boxing was a way to get some recognition and keep him out of trouble. When he began his amateur career, he won 85 straight bouts, 69 of them by knockout. There was little doubt that Walker Smith had talent, a lot of it.

He was still a teenager when he began fighting in "bootleg" bouts in upstate New York, getting paid as little as ten dollars a night. He had a manager then, George Gainford, who knew that his fighter was still too young to be licensed under his own name.

"George gave me this card with the name Ray Robinson on it," Sugar Ray recalled in later years. "It made me appear old enough to get a license. I always thought when I really turned pro I'd go back to my real name, but by then Sugar Walker Smith just didn't sound right."

So Sugar Ray Robinson it would be. He had his first professional fight on October 4, 1940, winning by a technical knockout over Joe Chevarria in two rounds. Four days later he was fighting again, knocking out someone named Silent Stafford in two rounds. By the end of the year he already had six fights. And in 1941, still not twenty years old, Ray Robinson began to campaign in earnest.

Back in those days there was no network television

to showcase glamorous young fighters. That meant no big paydays for even the best-looking youngsters. They had to work their way to the top the hard way—by fighting. While some of today's fighters find themselves being touted for title shots after 10 or 15 fights, the boxers from Sugar Ray Robinson's era had to serve a long apprenticeship. And they did it in the ring.

In 1941 alone Sugar Ray entered the ring a total of 20 times, winning each time and picking up the kind of valuable experience that enabled him to further harness his natural talents. In fact, by the end of April that year he already had ten fights. By the end of 1941 he was beginning to go up against better fighters. His final fight in 1941, and his first in January 1942, were both against Fritzie Zivic, who had held the world's welterweight championship for six months in 1941. Ray won them both.

After 14 more victories in 1942, bringing his record to 40–0, Sugar Ray met his first defeat. It was at the hands of a rough-tough brawler from New York, Jake LaMotta, who pounded out a ten-round decision on February 5, 1943. It was the first in an incredible six-fight series between the two fighters over an eight-year span. To show how often fighters entered the ring back then, Robinson and LaMotta met for a second time just three weeks after their first fight, and Ray quickly avenged his defeat with a ten-round decision of his own.

He beat Jake twice more in 1945. Finally, on December 20, 1945, after 62 victories, one loss, and a draw, and after some six years in the ring, Sugar Ray Robinson finally got his first world title. That was how long it took back then, and it happened in a strange way.

The 147-pound or welterweight champion was Marty Servo, who had won the crown on February 1, 1946. Later in the year Servo was forced to retire because of a nose ailment. After some debate, the New York State Boxing Commission tried to set up an elimination bout between Sugar Ray, considered the top contender, and several other prominent welterweights of the time. But by then everyone knew about the dynamite that Sugar carried in his fists, and a suitable opponent couldn't be found.

Finally the commission named Sugar Ray the new champion, and to make it official, they set up a bout between Ray and Tommy Bell on December 20. Sugar took a unanimous 15-round decision. He was a champion at last.

Sugar then dominated the welters for four years, defending his title only five times, but still fighting nontitle bouts almost very month, another thing unheard of for today's champions. He also began campaigning among the middleweights, and there was talk of his moving up to the 160-pound class. In June 1950 he won the vacant Pennsylvania Middleweight Championship, while still retaining his welter crown. He defended that crown twice, one of which was against Carl "Bobo" Olson, a slick fighter whom Sugar knocked out in 12 rounds.

Then in February of 1951 Sugar Ray climbed into the ring to try to capture the world middleweight title. Standing across the ring from him was the champion, none other than his old adversary, Jake LaMotta. The Bronx Bull, as LaMotta was called, took the title from Frenchman Marcel Cerdan in June 1949. So Jake had been the champ for a year and a half when he met Sugar Ray in Chicago.

In a battle more brutal than any of their previous

Sugar Ray won five out of six fights against tough Jake LaMotta. In this 1951 bout, Robinson won the middleweight title by stopping LaMotta on a technical knockout. (AP/Wide World Photos)

five fights, Sugar finally stopped LaMotta in the thirteenth round, becoming the middleweight king in the process. And after more than ten years in the ring, the man who was born Walker Smith finally had his due. Sugar Ray Robinson was being called one of the great ones.

Though he continued to fight nontitle bouts, a number of them during a tour of Europe, Sugar was enjoying the good life for the first time. And for the first time in his career he allowed himself to slip out of top shape. Despite a three-round TKO of Cyrille Delannoit in Italy on July 1, 1951, he wasn't the same Sugar when he defended his middleweight crown against Englishman Randy Turpin in London just nine days later. To the shock of the boxing world, Turpin pounded out a 15-round decision to take the title.

Now it was back to training in earnest. Sugar didn't fight at all until the return bout with Turpin on September 12 in New York. He was ready, and he was a solid favorite to regain the crown from the Englishman, who was a very competent, but not great, fighter. Robinson was already thirty years old, Turpin just twenty-two. The loss to Turpin had just been the second of Sugar's long career.

Turpin used his youth and strength to keep the fight close through nine rounds, though most fans still felt Sugar's superior boxing skills would win out. But then in the tenth round everything changed. The Englishman opened a dangerous gash over Sugar's eye. If the cut couldn't be closed, there was a good chance the fight would be stopped and Turpin would be declared the winner.

As the bell sounded for the eleventh round, one writer described what happened.

"What followed was the other side of Sugar Ray," he wrote. "Now there were no flashing feet. Now there was only Robinson walking straight ahead into the den of a fighter who sensed the end of a legend. Two straight right hands turned the fight around."

Turpin went down from the second right, and when he got up, Sugar moved in and quickly finished the job, hitting the Englishman with such rapidity that the referee had to stop it. Not only had Ray regained his title, but he had shown the ability to reach deep down inside himself for that little extra needed to win in any situation. Only the great ones have that kind of talent.

The next year Ray successfully defended his title against Carl "Bobo" Olson and Rocky Graziano. Then, at the end of June, he made his try for the light-heavyweight crown and was KO'd by the heat and humidity. After pondering his future for a few months, he surprised everyone by announcing his retirement from boxing.

It seemed a logical move. He had had a lot of fights, and was thirty-one now. By that time he was already being called one of the greatest ever. Plus Sugar Ray had a second love. Dancing. He felt he could make dancing a second career, and that's what he tried to do. At first he appeared in clubs and on television. He was a sports celebrity and people wanted to see him.

But it didn't take long for the novelty of Ray Robinson the dancer to wear off. While he was an exceptional performer in boxing, his dancing was merely good. He wasn't about to be a superstar on the dance floor. As the bookings decreased, money began getting short. Finally, on October 20, 1954, Ray announced he was returning to the ring.

His first comeback fight was on January 5, 1955, when he knocked out Joe Rindone in six rounds. Though he lost his next fight to the solid Ralph "Tiger" Jones, he was beginning to show flashes of the old skills. Four more bouts and he was ready. In December he regained the middleweight crown for the third time, and he did it by knocking out old adversary Bobo Olson in just two rounds.

This marked the beginning of the final phase of Ray's long career. Because of his declining skills, he would be involved in more epic battles, fights he would undoubtedly have won with ease ten years earlier. Now the big fights were often struggles, though he still had the ability to become the old Sugar Ray for maybe a round or two, or for part of a round. When that happened, he was still extremely dangerous.

Sugar fought just twice in 1956 and three times in 1957, a far cry from earlier years. But all three fights in 1957 were classics. In January Ray lost his title to Gene Fullmer, an unorthodox brawler from Utah. It was a hard-fought, 15-round decision. Then there was a return match in May, and most experts felt Fullmer was just too strong for the almost thirty-six-year-old Robinson.

That was how it looked for four rounds. In the fifth Sugar suddenly unleashed a left hook that caught the charging Fullmer flush on the jaw. The Utah fighter was knocked down and out. Even today, Sugar's "perfect punch" is talked about as one of the best one-punch knockouts in ring annals. It also enabled Ray to take back the middleweight title for the fourth time.

"He was a good fighter, probably one of the best," Gene Fullmer would say. "He was rangy. And he was fast, quick, and smart. I always admired Ray. He was a classy fighter.''

With his middleweight crown back, Ray signed to meet the welterweight champion, Carmen Basilio. Basilio was a battler, a never-say-die kind of fighter who could hit with either hand. He and Sugar met in December of 1957 for the first time. It was an epic battle, an action-packed fight for 15 rounds. Both fighters were bruised and battered when it ended, and Basilio won a close, split decision to take the title.

Again, many thought Ray should quit. But he signed to meet Basilio in a return match the following March. Once again the two fighters traded blows for the full 15 rounds. Basilio had to fight the last rounds with his left eye completely closed, and when this one ended, it was Sugar Ray Robinson who won a split decision. And he had made history by taking home the middleweight title for an unprecedented fifth time.

But age and ring weariness were starting to show. Ray fought just once in 1958—the second fight with Basilio—and once in 1959. Finally the National Boxing Association stripped him of his title, though some other boxing organizations still recognized him. But then he lost the remaining part of his title on a 15-round decision to a journeyman fighter named Paul Pender. And when he tried to regain it, he lost another 15-round decision.

He would also fight Gene Fullmer twice more for Fullmer's NBA title. The two fought a draw in December 1960, then in March 1961 Fullmer won a tough, 15-round decision. It would be the last title fight Sugar Ray would have. Now he would certainly quit.

But he didn't. He still needed the money—and maybe the attention—that fighting provided. Instead

One of the great fighters of the modern era, Sugar Ray Leonard (left, in his victory over Marvelous Marvin Hagler) admits freely that he took his nickname in homage to the master, Sugar Ray Robinson. (Courtesy HBO)

of fighting less, he fought more, often going against youngsters and journeymen who didn't belong in the same ring with him. That was when he picked up most of his 19 losses. He fought ten times in both 1963 and 1964. Then came 1965.

As unbelievable as it might seem, Sugar Ray entered the ring 16 times in 1965, when he was forty-four years old. He was fighting as often as he had twenty-four years earlier. To some it was sad, almost tragic. In October, for instance, he was in Johnstown, Pennsylvania, to fight Peter Schmidt, the welterweight champion of Canada.

For six rounds the two fought a close battle. Sugar was a shell of his former self, but still able to go through the motions. But as he came out for the seventh, something clicked. He suddenly landed six straight jabs. Then he hooked off the jab twice and followed it quickly with a right cross that drove Schmidt into the ropes. The crowd went wild, and Sugar took a deep breath.

The flurry over, he went back to being a forty-four-year-old fighter and just barely won a ten-round decision. For those few seconds in the seventh round he had turned back the clock, and he knew it.

"I wanted to show them something," he said after the fight. "I wanted to give them whatever I had left. I know I couldn't go beyond that, but I had to at least give them that."

Sugar only got $1,500 that night. That was what he was fighting for then. Two months later, after losing a decision to light-punching Joey Archer, he finally called it quits for the last time. Just two years later he was elected to the Boxing Hall of Fame.

Still handsome, and relatively unmarked after all those fights, things got better for Sugar in retirement.

Former star athletes were more in demand during the 1970s, and he was a much admired figure throughout the sports world. He also spent a great deal of time working with kids in the ghetto areas of Los Angeles, and started the very successful Sugar Ray Robinson Youth Foundation.

By then Sugar was no longer bitter about the things that had happened to him to force him to stay in the ring too long.

"I had the best," he said. "I got no regrets, not even for the bad times, the hurtin' times."

Ray was a popular figure at all the big fights into the 1980s. In the late eighties he didn't seem the same to his old friends. Something was wrong. Then it was learned that he was suffering from Alzheimer's disease, the one opponent not even Sugar Ray Robinson could lick. He died on April 12, 1989, and the boxing world and the world at large mourned his passing.

"He was the greatest I ever saw," said longtime boxing matchmaker Teddy Brenner. "But fighting all those years, that would be too much for anybody. Today a guy has 30 fights and he has already won four of those so-called titles.

"Ali and Robinson were alike in their graceful moves," Brenner continued, "but the big difference was that Robinson could knock you out with either hand. He was a great puncher, and Ali wasn't."

The accolades came from all over. Fight fans will never forget the fights with LaMotta, with Fullmer, with Basilio. And they won't forget the young Robinson, the flash and dash, followed by the lightning bolts in his fists. The sad part is that he didn't fight in another era, one that would have allowed him to leave when he was ready. But as Sugar himself said, he had no regrets.

Of all the praise heaped upon Sugar Ray Robinson, perhaps the best testimony came from the late Cus D'Amato, who managed both Floyd Patterson and Mike Tyson. To emphasize his feeling that Sugar was the greatest ever, D'Amato said: "There's Sugar Ray, and then there's the top ten."

3

THE 1969–70 NEW YORK KNICKS
A Team of Champions

At the outset of the 1969–70 National Basketball Association season, everyone knew a change was in the air. The reason was simple. Bill Russell had retired. While the great center of the Boston Celtics wasn't a one-man team, he was the anchor around whom the Celtics revolved. And with Russell in the middle, the Celts had dominated pro basketball in a way no other team has dominated its sport, with the possible exception of the New York Yankees in baseball.

The Celtics became the NBA's best team the day the 6′9″ Russell joined them out of the University of San Francisco in 1956. They won the championship in 1956–57, and would win it a total of 11 times in 13 seasons, including an incredible eight in a row from 1958–59 to 1965–66. In 1968–69 the Celts and the aging Russell finished fourth in the regular season, but turned back the clock in the playoffs and whipped the Los Angeles Lakers in seven games for yet another title. Then Russell retired.

Boston had been a great team. But with Russell

gone, it was common knowledge that the club just wasn't powerful enough to challenge again in 1969–70. The question then was which team would emerge as the new champion? Even before the Russell era, the NBA champion usually featured a big man, a star center who could dominate the action. Big George Mikan did the job for the old Minneapolis Lakers in the early days of the league. Then came Russell and his chief rival, Wilt Chamberlain. It was Wilt and the Philadelphia 76ers who managed to dethrone the Celts after eight straight titles in 1966–67.

Wilt was still playing with the Los Angeles Lakers in 1969, but would injure a knee and be lost for the year after just 12 games. Then there were the Milwaukee Bucks. They had just acquired the most talked-about rookie in recent years, 7′2″ Lew Alcindor—later known as Kareem Abdul-Jabbar—who had led the UCLA Bruins to three straight national championships. Would the Bucks be the team to rise to the top?

Finally there were the New York Knickerbockers. The Knicks were a team on the rise. After being a last-place, 30–50 team in 1965–66, the New Yorkers had topped the .500 mark for the first time in years during the 1967–68 season, finishing third in their division with a 43–39 mark. A year later the team was third again, but this time with a fine 54–28 record that left them just three games out of first place. Though they lost to the Celtics in the semifinals of the playoffs, they had become the top defensive team in the league and had to be considered a threat in 1969–70. While the team was already a known commodity, no one was really prepared for what was about to happen.

It all began in the second half of the previous season, shortly after the most important trade in the

Center Willis Reed was the captain of the Knicks and the team's inspirational leader as well. When healthy, the big guy from Grambling could compete with anyone. (Courtesy Basketball Hall of Fame)

history of the franchise. The team had started the year with 6'11" Walt Bellamy at center and 6'9" Willis Reed at forward. Reed had joined the Knicks in 1964–65 out of Grambling College, and as a rookie center had averaged 19.5 points and grabbed 1,175 rebounds, good enough to be named Rookie of the Year.

However, before the next season began, the team picked up Bellamy in a trade and moved Reed to power forward. "Big Bells" had joined the expansionist Chicago franchise in 1961, and as a rookie was second in the league in scoring behind Chamberlain, averaging 31.6 points a game, and third in rebounding behind Wilt and Russell. He seemed on the brink of becoming the game's next great center.

But after that, Bellamy's play became spotty. Some nights he came to play—others he seemed to be somewhere else. Even so, the Knicks picked him up in the hope that he could regain the intensity of his rookie year. While Reed adjusted to the forward slot, Big Bells wasn't the answer in the middle. Reed, however, was big and tough, a no-nonsense player who gave a hundred percent every single night he played. As one of the league's coaches commented back then, "If I had a choice, I'd take Reed over any other forward in the league. Then, I'd play him at center."

That's what the Knicks decided to do in December 1968. They sent Bellamy and guard Howard Komives to Detroit for a 6'6" forward named Dave DeBusschere. With Reed back in the middle and DeBusschere fitting in with the others, the Knicks became a team and played as well as anyone for the remainder of the season.

So when 1969–70 rolled around, they were ready to make their move. The team had a lot more going for it than just Willis Reed and Dave DeBusschere. The playmaker was 6′4″ Walt "Clyde" Frazier, a slick guard out of Southern Illinois who had joined the Knicks in 1967. It took about a year for Frazier to get the feel of the pro game, but once he did, he really asserted himself. Frazier was a solid ballhandler, passer, and scorer. On top of that, he had become perhaps the best defensive guard in the NBA, capable of making key steals at any time. He loved that aspect of the game.

"After I've made a steal, I'm really keyed up," Frazier once said. "For the next three or four minutes I might just go wild, in spurts. I like to hear the cheers of the crowd. It really psychs me up."

The other starting guard was veteran Dick Barnett, a deadly left-handed shooter who often took a backseat to Frazier, but a player who could also do it all. Reed and DeBusschere did the dirty work underneath. Both were rebounders who could also score, and they worked exceedingly well together.

The fifth starter was 6′5″ forward Bill Bradley, who today is a United States Senator from New Jersey. Back then Bradley was an all-American out of Princeton who returned to the NBA after a stay at Oxford University in England as a Rhodes scholar. Bradley never became the same kind of superstar in the pros that he had been in college. But he was an extremely intelligent player who loved the team concept and blended in perfectly with the philosophy of the Knicks, as imparted by their coach, William "Red" Holzman.

The team was also solid off the bench. The sixth man was 6′5″ Cazzie Russell, a great all-American from Michigan who was the team's top draft pick in 1966. Cazzie didn't pass or play team defense quite as well as Bradley, so Bill usually got the start. But Cazzie saw plenty of playing time and was capable of scoring points in explosive bunches.

Forward Dave Stallworth was another solid scorer off the bench, while scrappy Mike Riordan was a tenacious defender at the guard slot. Nate Bowman, at 6'10", could give Reed a breather at center, while youngsters Don May, Bill Hosket, and John Warren rounded out the squad.

It wasn't long before the rest of the NBA found out just how a good team could become great. It was that four letter word. T-E-A-M. That was the key. Red Holzman had the players he wanted, and he molded them into a ballclub that played exceedingly well together. They moved the ball unselfishly on offense. It didn't matter who got the points, as long as the job was done.

Defensively, the Knicks were superb, by far the best team in the league. Every player on the team worked hard at the defensive end. The rewards were victories, and the sellout crowds at New York's Madison Square Garden loved it, often chanting *"Defense, Defense, Defense"* when the ballclub really had it together. Though just 6'9", Willis Reed could block shots, and he battled for every rebound. DeBusschere, too, was a fine rebounder, often getting the ball before much taller men because of his position and tenacity.

Frazier was the catalyst, the man who made everything work because of his fast hands and ability to strip an opponent of the ball. He was the riverboat gambler who often took that extra chance if it meant disrupting the opposition's offense. And he knew that he had the others, especially Bradley, to back him up. Bradley explained how it worked:

"When Walt gambles and goes for the steal, I have

Walt "Clyde" Frazier gave the Knicks' title teams an all-around point guard who could handle the ball, pass, score, and play exciting defense. His quick hands turned many a game around and had Knicks fans chanting *"Defense, Defense, Defense."* (Courtesy Basketball Hall of Fame)

to take his man if he misses. If I don't, Walt looks bad, and if that happened often, he would lose confidence that I am there behind him. Eventually, he would stop gambling, and with that, our whole defense would fall apart."

It didn't. The Knicks came out of the gate like gangbusters. It was almost as if they ambushed the rest of the league. They were a team playing close to perfection, and that was the goal of Coach Holzman and his players. The team won its first six in a row before losing. If that wasn't enough to show the rest of the league they were for real, what they did next would.

They started to win again. Four, five, six wins in a row. Nine, ten, eleven straight. When the streak reached 15, it became the talk of basketball. The NBA record at that time was 17 straight victories—the Knicks were getting close. But even then there didn't seem to be any pressure, because the team was making it look easy.

"We didn't have that many nerve-racking games," Frazier said. "We were winning by 20 points or more, so this made it a lot easier than if we were just squeaking by. There might have been more pressure then, but the way we were winning, well, it was no big thing."

The record-tying win against Atlanta was the same kind of game. The Knicks led all the way, but really exploded in the fourth quarter, scoring 38 points to just 12 for the Hawks and winning 138–108. Two nights later they were in Cincinnati, trying to set a new NBA mark for consecutive victories. And this one wouldn't be easy at all. For one thing, Royals' coach Bob Cousy had been a member of the 1959 Celtics team that owned a piece of the record. He didn't want to see it broken against his ballclub.

Cousy, who was forty-one years old then and re-tired for seven years, had recently activated himself to try to light a fire under his team. He watched as the Royals played the Knicks tough all night. With just 1:49 left, the Royals led by three, 101–98. That was when Cincy star Oscar Robertson fouled out of the game. In a surprise move, Cousy inserted himself into the lineup, and for about a minute he turned back the clock. He threw a slick, crosscourt hook pass to guard Norm Van Lier for an open jumper and two points. Then the player-coach was fouled and hit both free throws. With 26 seconds left, the Royals had a 105–100 lead. It looked as if the streak was about to end.

But that was when the Knicks shifted into another gear and really showed what a great and opportunistic team they had become. First Reed was fouled trying to put in a rebound of a missed shot. He hit two free throws to make it 105–102. Seconds later DeBusschere stole a Cousy inbounds pass and dunked, cutting the Cincy lead to just a single point.

With time running down, the Royals only had to hold the ball. But the Knicks were pressing again. This time it was Reed, deflecting a pass and enabling Frazier to get it. Clyde started for the basket and threw up a shot that missed. But he had been fouled by Tom Van Arsdale while he was getting the shot off. With just two seconds left, he calmly made both free throws. The Royals couldn't get a shot off. The Knicks had won it, 106–105, setting a new NBA record of 18 consecutive victories.

The team won 26 of its first 28 games that season and seemed to have a stranglehold on the entire league. Perhaps it was the intensity of those first 28 games, perhaps just the league beginning to catch up with

Holzman's style of play, but their pace slowed somewhat after that, as they coasted home divisional champs. They were 34–20 the rest of the way, finishing at 60–22, just four games ahead of the Bucks and their great rookie, Lew Alcindor.

As the playoffs loomed ahead, there was still a question whether the Knicks would have the firepower to hold off Milwaukee. There also was another potential problem. Wilt Chamberlain, thought to be out for the year with knee surgery, had healed faster than anyone imagined and would rejoin the Lakers in time for the playoffs.

The first round would be a best of seven series against the tough Baltimore Bullets. The Bullets matched up well with the Knicks. They had young Wes Unseld at center. He was just 6'8", but tough as nails, a good rebounder who threw a lightning-fast outlet pass to put his team on offense.

Earl "The Pearl" Monroe was a 6'3" guard and the team's leading scorer, a dynamic player who could put on a one-man show when hot. Gus Johnson was a physical power forward, much like DeBusschere; and Jack Marin, nearly a 20-point scorer, was at the other forward.

The series was close all the way. The lead changed hands back and forth in the opener, both teams taking turns on top. Monroe astounded the crowd with 39 big points, while Unseld swept the boards to the tune of 31 rebounds. But Reed had countered with 21 rebounds and 30 points, while DeBusschere and Bradley each had more than 20. Fittingly, the game went into overtime, then a second overtime. With Frazier making four steals in OT, the Knicks finally prevailed, 120–117.

That one set the tone. The two teams struggled for

the full seven games. In the final, pressure-packed contest played before 19,500 fans at Madison Square Garden, the Knicks prevailed, 127–114. When it was over, it was Walt Frazier who explained what playoff pressure was all about:

"The guy who comes up with ten baskets in the last quarter of a regular-season game when his team is leading or trailing by 30 points is probably not going to be all that great when the pressure is on," Clyde said. "It's the man who wants to handle the ball in every clutch situation that you really need; the guy who wants to take the key shot or go for the key steal. He's the one who will win a playoff for you."

Now it was Alcindor and the Bucks in the conference final. Milwaukee was a maturing team that had whipped Philadelphia in five games in round one. Alcindor was already a force in the middle, while guard Flynn Robinson and forward Bob Dandridge provided the club with balanced scoring.

Instead of going shot for shot with the Bucks, the cerebral Knicks again used sound strategy and a team concept. Since Reed was a strong outside shooter, he drew young Alcindor away from the basket and out of rebounding position. Frazier knew that Flynn Robinson wasn't a strong ballhandler, and kept forcing him to go left, taking much of his offense away.

The result was a surprisingly easy Knicks victory. They whipped the Bucks in five games, including a 132–96 trouncing in the clincher. Now the club was in the final against the Los Angeles Lakers and their trio of superstars: Chamberlain, guard Jerry West, and Forward Elgin Baylor. The three were considered all-time greats even then.

Game One was held on April 24, 1970, at Madison Square Garden. Once again the Knicks used their basketball brains. Though Reed was willing to battle the taller Chamberlain underneath, he also moved outside and popped for a game-high 37 points. At the same time, Frazier did a stellar defensive job on the slick West. The Knicks took a big lead early and went on to win, 124–112.

West was the hero of the second game. One of the great clutch performers in basketball history, the former West Virginia all-American scored 34 points. But it was his two free throws in the closing seconds that clinched a 105–103 victory to even the series at one game apiece. By winning at Madison Square Garden, the Lakers had taken the home-court advantage away from the Knicks.

The two teams flew to Los Angeles for Game Three. It was another close one all the way. Just when it seemed as if the Knicks had it won, West made a desperate 55-foot shot to tie the game. But in the overtime the Knicks kept their poise and won it, 111–108. The fourth game also went into OT. This time it was the Lakers who won, with West scoring 37 points, Baylor 30, and Wilt grabbing 25 rebounds. Dick Barnett had 29 for the Knicks.

So it was back to New York with the series tied at two games each. Then, in the first quarter of the fifth game, an unexpected injury would give the rest of the series a dramatic impact that is still talked about today. Near the end of the period, with the Lakers holding a 25–15 lead, Willis Reed fell very hard to the floor on a drive to the hoop. And he wasn't getting up. He finally limped off the court, two muscles in his right thigh severely strained. He wouldn't be back.

With their captain out, the Knicks really had to pull together as a team. They ran, pressed, harassed, and double-teamed the Lakers. Their defense was almost

When the Knicks traded for forward Dave DeBusschere, they got an unselfish player who would do anything for the team. He was considered the final piece to the puzzle that resulted in a championship ballclub. (Courtesy Basketball Hall of Fame)

incredible. On no less than thirty occasions, a veteran Laker team with three superstars came downcourt and failed to get off a shot. There was either a turnover, violation, or steal by the Knicks. Even the Knicks bench contributed to the onslaught. When the game ended, the Knicks had an incredible 107–100 victory. Without Reed, they had taken a 3–2 lead in the series.

Back in Los Angeles for Game Six, the Knicks found themselves once again playing without Reed, the man who kept opponents honest. One NBA veteran told of the respect and fear opponents had for the Knicks center:

"I once hit Reed in the mouth with my elbow as I came down with a rebound, and I apologized fast . . . as quick as I could get it out of my mouth. I remembered almost hooking up with Willis earlier in the year, and he said to me then, 'I own this court when I'm out here. I'm the king bee.' I knew he meant it."

But without Reed in there, could the Knicks pull off another miracle? This time they couldn't. The Lakers had regrouped and changed their game plan. They handled the pressure defense and won easily, 135–113. Now it was back to New York for the seventh and deciding game. And the question on everyones' lips was the same: Would Willis Reed be able to play?

There was no announcement before the game. The rest of the Knicks came out to warm up and the crowd was almost silent. There was still no Willis Reed. Then, shortly before the tip-off, the big guy made his way out of the locker room. He was wearing his warmups, and the crowd went wild. They continued to roar as the Knicks captain threw up a couple of practice shots. Though he was moving gingerly on the bad leg, he wanted to play. Even the Lakers were watching his every move.

He was out there as the game began. On the Knicks' first possession, Reed trailed the play, took a pass, and hit a jumper. The crowd went wild again. Minutes later he hit his second shot and the adrenaline seemed to shoot through the crowd and the rest of the Knicks players. Though he couldn't move well, the big guy also leaned on Chamberlain inside, doing his best to keep Wilt away from the basket.

In the second quarter the captain limped off the court to a standing ovation. He wouldn't return, but by then the Knicks had a healthy lead. And they were using the same tactics as they had in Game Five, harassing the Lakers all over the court, with Coach Holzman running fresh players in and out of the game. Walt Frazier was playing the game of his life, scoring and setting up teammates with his passes. By halftime the Knicks had an almost unbelievable 69–42 lead.

Whenever the Lakers tried to close the gap in the second half, Frazier would take charge again. Though the lead began narrowing in the final session, there was never a real serious doubt about the outcome. The final buzzer was the one that made the New York Knickerbockers champions. They won the game, 113–99, and had done it against the likes of Chamberlain, West, and Baylor, with Willis Reed scoring only four early points and spending most of the night on the bench.

Frazier had done the most damage, with 36 points and a record-tying 19 assists. DeBusschere had 18 points and 17 rebounds, while Barnett added 21 and Bradley 17. But most of all it was a team effort, just as the entire season had been. It takes outstanding individuals to make a team, but they have to want it to be that way.

The 1969–70 Knicks did, and they played the game the way it was meant to be played. In a way, their victory—the first after the end of the Celtics' dynasty—paved the way for others who followed. In the ensuing years it was often the team that played together and rose to the occasion that emerged the winner. True pro sports champions.

4

GIANTS vs. COLTS
The Greatest Game Ever Played

The year was 1958, and the National Football League was far from the huge, big-money spectacle that it is today. Vince Lombardi hadn't even become coach of the Packers then, the American Football League hadn't started play, and the Super Bowl was still nearly a decade away. But there was a championship game that year that some people insist marked the beginning of the pro football explosion that continues today.

There were just 12 teams in the NFL back then, and the regular season consisted of 12 games, not the 16 played today. In addition, there were no playoffs unless two teams were tied for first place. There was just one championship game between the Eastern and Western Conference winners.

That didn't mean there weren't some very great players in the NFL at the time. With just 12 teams, only the very best made it to the pros. It was a competitive business, and many of those who made it were among the greatest ever to play the game. In fact, during the 1958 regular season, the incomparable

Jim Brown of the Cleveland Browns set a new rushing mark with 1,527 yards.

In Baltimore a young quarterback named John Unitas was helping to bring respectability to a franchise that had been down and out for years. And in New York the Giants had a rock-ribbed defense, led by a dynamic middle linebacker named Sam Huff, that inspired the fans as much as the offense. The chant of *"Defense, Defense, Defense"* often cascaded down from the far reaches of Yankee Stadium when Huff and his teammates were on the field. The entire defensive unit that year helped bring recognition and glamour to a part of the sport that was often taken for granted and neglected by the fans.

So it was an exciting season in many ways, and that excitement continued right down to the final weeks of the campaign. In the Western Conference it was a three-team race between the Colts, the Chicago Bears, and Los Angeles Rams. Led by Unitas, who had been an unwanted quarterback after coming out of the University of Louisville—he was unceremoniously cut by the Steelers—the Colts took an early lead in the race.

Johnny U, as he was called, had a pair of outstanding pass receivers in Raymond Berry and flanker Lenny Moore, and a solid tight end in Jim Mutscheller. Alan "The Horse" Ameche was a bruising fullback, and L. G. Dupre a solid halfback. The offensive line, led by big Jim Parker and Alex Sandusky, also did a fine job.

Defensively the Colts were also very strong, especially on the line and in its linebacking corps. Gene "Big Daddy" Lipscomb and Art Donovan were huge tackles, while end Gino Marchetti was an All-Pro. Don Shinnick and Bill Pellington were outstanding linebackers, while the secondary was also solid.

But with all these elements, it was still the leadership and ability of Unitas that elevated the team to the top. The Colts won their first five games that year and were handily winning the sixth against Green Bay when potential disaster struck. A Packer player fell on Unitas's back with his knees, leaving the quarterback with fractured ribs and a punctured lung. It was feared he might be lost for the season.

Veteran backup George Shaw finished the 56–0 rout, but the next week the Colts went up against the Giants. Although Shaw threw for three scores, linebacker Huff intercepted a key pass late in the game to preserve a 24–21 Giants victory. Then in a head-to-head meeting with the second-place Bears, the Baltimore defense dominated and the Colts won, 17–0.

The next week Unitas came back wearing a special steel and foam-rubber harness to protect his ribs. When he led his club to a 34–7 triumph over the Rams, Baltimore fans breathed a sigh of relief. The week after, against the 49ers, Unitas really showed his magic. At the half the Colts found themselves trailing, 27–7. Fans remembered the team fading in the final games the year before and hoped it wouldn't happen again.

It didn't. Unitas and company put 28 second-half points on the board and won it, 35–27, clinching the Western Conference title with two games still remaining. Even though they lost both, they wound up conference champions at 9–3 and turned to watch the East.

In the East it was long-time power Cleveland and the rival New York Giants going head to head for the title. When they met midway through the season, the Giants had prevailed, 21–17, but coming into the final game of the season, Cleveland had a 9–2 record, and

Quarterback John Unitas of the Baltimore Colts took a giant step toward greatness in the 1958 NFL championship game. Not only did Unitas bring his team from behind in regulation time, but he was brilliant and daring in the sudden-death overtime period that resulted in the Colts' 23–17 victory. Johnny U would eventually wind up in the Pro Football Hall of Fame, with many still calling him the greatest ever. (Courtesy Indianapolis Colts)

the Giants were at 8–3. That meant the New Yorkers needed a victory to force a playoff game for the championship.

The New York offense featured the likes of quarterback Charley Conerly, running backs Frank Gifford, Alex Webster, and Mel Triplett, receivers Kyle Rote and Bob Schnelker. And they operated behind a solid offensive line. But many felt it was the defense that made the team go. Tom Landry was the defensive coach. He would later coach the Dallas Cowboys for more than a quarter of a century. Landry was credited with being the first to use the 4–3 formation.

In 1958 he had the men to do it. His tackles were Dick Modzelewski and Rosey Grier, the ends Andy Robustelli and Jim Katcavage. Huff, Harland Svare, and Cliff Livingston were the linebackers, and the defensive backfield had Emlen Tunnell, Jim Patton, Lindon Crow, and Carl Karilivacz. They made a great defensive unit.

The final game of the regular season was played on a snow-swept field at Yankee Stadium in New York. Cleveland drew first blood in the opening period when the great Jim Brown broke one right over the middle and ran 65 yards for a touchdown. The Giants came back with a 41-yard Pat Summerall field goal to make the score 7–3 after one. Then Cleveland kicker Lou "The Toe" Groza booted one 33 yards in the second period, making it 10–3.

It stayed that way right through the third quarter. As the weather got worse, the Giants' defense seemed to get better. The question was whether the offense could pull it out in the fourth period. At halftime Kyle Rote had told quarterback Conerly that the Cleveland secondary might be vulnerable to the halfback option because they kept coming up fast to stop the sweep.

"We sat on that play waiting for the right time," Frank Gifford said. "Finally, with about five minutes left, Charley [Conerly] figured it was the right time."

The Giants had recovered a Jim Brown fumble on the Cleveland 45-yard line. On the first play, Conerly pitched out to Gifford, who faked a sweep, then fired a pass to Rote, who grabbed it and was caught from behind at the six. Three plays later they did it again, Gifford throwing to Bob Schnelker for the touchdown. Summerall's kick tied the score at 10–10. But the Giants needed more. There was no overtime period then except in the championship game, and a tie would give the Browns the conference title.

Cleveland couldn't move the ball, and a punt gave the Giants the football at midfield. Conerly drove his ballclub to the 29 and Summerall came on to try a field goal from the 36. He missed it badly to the left. Not surprisingly, he felt his flubbed kick had cost the Giants the crown.

Again the Giants' defense held and the Browns had to punt. It was snowing once more as the Giants started from near midfield. Conerly tried a long pass to Alex Webster, but he dropped it on the one. Finally it was fourth and long from the Cleveland 42. Offensive coach Vince Lombardi wanted Conerly to throw, but head coach Jim Lee Howell looked at Summerall and said, "'Go for it."

The veteran placekicker set up at the 49. The goalposts were right on the goal line then, so it would be a 49-yard kick. With the snow coming down, Charley Conerly took the snap and placed the ball down. Summerall swung his leg through, head down, perfect form.

"As soon as I hit it, I knew it would be far enough,"

said Summerall. "I watched it all the way until I could see that it was inside the left upright."

The kick was good and the Giants' fans went wild. There was just 2:07 left, and the New York defense did the rest. The Giants won it, 13–10, forcing a playoff for the title the following week, the winner meeting the Colts for the NFL championship.

It was the Giants' defense that dominated the extra game. Cleveland couldn't get anything started the entire afternoon, and when it ended, the New Yorkers had a 10–0 victory and the conference title. Some experts were quick to point out that the two tough games with Cleveland probably tired the Giants' players, but others figured the sensational wins over the Browns would have the team sky-high for the title tilt. With their beloved defense and veteran offense, New York fans considered their ball club a team of destiny.

The championship game was played at Yankee Stadium on December 28, 1958, and the Giants were heavy favorites. As good as the Colts were all year, they were not considered to be in the same class as Cleveland, and the Giants had beaten the Browns three times. Despite the great season turned in by the twenty-five-year-old Unitas, the youngster was still not widely considered among the quarterback elite in the NFL.

More than 64,000 fans jammed into Yankee Stadium for the big game, and one of the largest national television audiences ever to see a football game also tuned in as the two teams squared off. The Giants' defense did the job during the first ten minutes of the game, but found themselves matched by the Baltimore defenders. Neither team could manage a first down.

It was the Colts who mounted the first threat of the game. Unitas hit speedy Lenny Moore on a slant-in, and the former Penn State star grabbed the ball at the New York 40 and carried it all the way to the 25. Once again the Giants defense dug in and stopped the Colts. When Steve Myhra tried to boot a field goal, Huff managed to block it and the fans went wild.

Then the Giants struck quickly. A pass to fullback Mel Triplett brought the ball from the 20 to the 31. From there, halfback Gifford broke one, rambling 38 yards to the Colts' 31. When the Baltimore defense stiffened, it was Pat Summerall again, this time booting a 36-yarder to give the Giants a 3–0 lead.

But in the second quarter the complexion of the game suddenly changed. It started when tackle Big Daddy Lipscomb recovered a Gifford fumble inside the Giants' 20-yard line. Unitas came on and surprised everyone by keeping the ball on the ground. Ameche and Moore ran right at the New York defense with Ameche finally hammering in from the two. Myhra's kick made it a 7–3 game.

When the Giants threatened again toward the end of the quarter, the usually reliable Gifford coughed the ball up a second time, this one on the Baltimore 14. Once again Unitas had his team driving, and once more he kept the ball mainly on the ground. Maybe he was trying to wear down the Giants' defense. He threw only twice during the drive, both times to top receiver Raymond Berry. The second pass was good for a 15-yard touchdown. The kick made it 14–3, and that's the way the half ended, with the New York fans looking on in disbelief.

With just 30 minutes of football left, the Giants would have to rally. Baltimore Coach Weeb Ewbank tried to keep his club high. It looked like it would happen when the Colts took the kickoff and marched straight downfield, getting a first and goal at the Giants' three. Then three times the Colts tried to run it over, and three times the Giants held. With a fourth and goal coming, a field goal would have been almost automatic.

"We talked about going for a field goal," Coach Ewbank said, "but I wanted to bury them right there with a touchdown."

It was sound thinking, but it didn't work. As soon as fullback Ameche got the ball, linebacker Cliff Livingston slammed into him for a four-yard loss. It was a memorable goal-line stand, the kind that turns the momentum of a game. Now the Giants' offense was ready to take advantage of it. And they quickly got a big break.

A pair of running plays brought the ball to the 13. Then Conerly dropped back and hit Rote at the Baltimore 40. Rote started upfield but was hit hard from behind at the 25 by defensive back Andy Nelson. The ball popped loose, but not for long. Alex Webster was trailing the play and picked up the loose pigskin without breaking stride. By the time the Colts caught the big halfback, he was at the one-yard line. From there Mel Triplett bulled in for the score. Summerall's kick closed the gap to 14–10.

At the outset of the fourth quarter the Giants began moving again. The wily Conerly knew the Colts would be watching Gifford and Rote closely, so he began going instead to tight end Schnelker. First he hit the veteran receiver for 17 yards, then went right back to him for a big gainer of 46 yards, bringing the ball to the Baltimore 15. From there Conerly spotted Gifford and drilled it home for another score. The kick made it 17–14. The Giants had taken the lead and seemed to have things their way.

Now the defense was all over Unitas. They stopped a pair of potential Baltimore drives, then took the ball with less than three minutes left. A first down and they might be able to eat up the clock and win the game. It came down to a third and four at their own 40. Conerly gave the ball to Gifford, who sliced off right tackle. He was stopped by Marchetti and Lipscomb, but for a split second seemed to make the first down. However, when the ref spotted the ball, he moved it back a bit and the measurement came up just short.

On the play, Gino Marchetti fractured his leg and had to be carried from the field. But the big defensive end refused to leave the sideline and seek medical aid. He wanted to watch the end of the game, and in doing so helped inspire his teammates. He watched as the Giants elected to punt on fourth and inches. Don Chandler booted one high and deep, and the Colts had to fair catch at their own 14.

"I'd have done the same thing," said assistant coach Vince Lombardi of Coach Howell's decision to kick. "Chandler's punt was a beauty, and with the Colts back at their 14, I was sure it was over."

But as they say so often, it ain't over till it's over. John Unitas was about to come of age in front of 64,000 fans and millions of television viewers. He remembered how psyched he and his teammates were.

"We were so disgusted with ourselves that when we got the ball for that last series, we struck back at the Giants in a sort of blind fury," he said.

The first test came with a third and ten situation. Unitas dropped back and calmly hit Moore at the 25 for a first down. On the very next play Johnny U went to Raymond Berry over the middle for 25 more. Then Berry took over the heroics with a diving catch at the Giants' 35-yard line. From there Berry ran a hook pattern and Unitas found him at the 13.

There were just 30 seconds left, so the Colts sent out Myhra to try a 20-yard field goal to knot the game. At the snap, the huge crowd hoped for a block, then a miss. But the kick was right through the uprights. The Colts had made a clutch drive in the closing seconds to tie the game at 17–17. As the clock ran down, football fans everywhere realized they were about to witness something that had never happened before in National Football League annals. The Giants and Colts would be playing the first ever sudden-death overtime title game.

It started with another coin toss, which the Giants won. Since the first team to score in any way would win the game, New York elected to receive. Once again the fans began tuning up, hoping their heroes could march down the field and ring up either a field goal or touchdown. Don Maynard returned the kickoff to the 20, where Conerly and company took over.

But after a run by Gifford went nowhere and a pass fell incomplete, Conerly dropped back again. Though by no means a running quarterback, the veteran saw an opening up the middle and took it. For a split second it appeared he would run for a first down, but the Colts nailed him less than a yard short. Again the Giants chose not to gamble, but to punt. Once more Don Chandler came through, booming one all the way down to the Baltimore 20.

Out came Unitas once again. He was hoping to mount a sustained drive. "I wanted to move the ball on the ground to minimize any chance of losing the ball," he said.

L. G. Dupre started it with an 11-yard jaunt for a first down. Then on a third and eight, Ameche caught

60

a short pass for a first. Facing yet another third-down play, Unitas dropped back quickly and looked for his favorite target. Raymond Berry was open and nailed the pass for a 21-yard gain.

Showing poise and cleverness beyond his years, Unitas then crossed up the veteran Giants' defense. Knowing they were looking for another pass, Johnny U gave the ball to Ameche on a draw play and The Horse charged up the middle for 23 big yards, bringing the ball to the Giants' 21.

At this point Ewbank could have elected to have Myhra attempt a field goal for the win. But both coach and quarterback decided to try to get even closer. After a sweep by Dupre gained nothing, Unitas went back to the air and to Raymond Berry. Sure enough, Berry was open and grabbed the ball at the eight-yard line. Now the Giants were in deep trouble.

But instead of kicking the field goal, surely an easy chip shot, Unitas went upstairs again. He hit Jim Mutscheller at the one. Now Yankee Stadium was hushed to an eerie silence. It was almost as if time had stopped as Unitas brought the Colts to the line of scrimmage. The Giants dug in, hoping to postpone what seemed inevitable. But Unitas merely gave the ball to his fullback, and Alan Ameche slammed into the end zone. It was over.

The Colts had done it, won the game by a 23–17 count in sudden-death overtime, some eight minutes and 15 seconds into the extra period.

"When I slapped the ball into Ameche's belly and saw him take off, I knew nobody was going to stop him," said Unitas, who had completed 26 of 40 passes for 349 yards. The omnipresent Berry had caught 12 of them for 178 yards. But the important thing was that the Baltimore Colts were world champions!

One of the great moments in pro football history is captured on film as Baltimore Colts fullback Alan "The Horse" Ameche (lower left, clutching football) plunges into the end zone for the winning touchdown in the 1958 NFL championship game. The Colts beat the New York Giants in the first sudden-death title game in NFL history. Number 70 in the dark helmet is the Giants' great middle linebacker, Sam Huff, and number 45 in the dark jersey is Giants All-Pro safety, Emlen Tunnell. (Courtesy Indianapolis Colts)

The greatest game ever played? Probably not artistically. But it might have had the greatest impact on its sport. For the huge national television audience that day saw an event of unparalleled drama. And they loved it. The Giants and Colts would play a return engagement the next year, and the year after that Vince Lombardi—who took over the Packers in 1959—would have the Pack in the title game. Professional football was really on its way, thanks to a quarterback that nobody wanted and a pass receiver nobody could stop.

Unitas, Berry, and the Baltimore Colts were surely pro sports champions.

5

KAREEM ABDUL-JABBAR

A Champion in Every Way

Any athlete who competes for 20 years in his sport has to be considered special. But an athlete who can compete for two decades and be dominant most of that time, well, he comes along maybe once in a lifetime. Baseball's Ty Cobb was such a player. So was Gordie Howe in hockey. Pitcher Nolan Ryan, still active going into 1990, also qualifies as a very special player.

Ask the same question about professional basketball and there can be only one answer. Kareem Abdul-Jabbar. Not only did the 7'2" center of the Milwaukee Bucks and Los Angeles Lakers set an NBA mark by playing from 1969–70 through the 1988–89 season, but he was a dominant performer from the first day he entered the league until perhaps just a year prior to his retirement. Yet even in his final season he was a lot more than an embarrassment. He could still be a force on occasions. It's just that the occasions didn't come as frequently.

Abdul-Jabbar is also considered a link to the past,

the last of the great centers who dominated the sport since the NBA was formed in the middle 1940s. While there are still some great big men today, such as Patrick Ewing and Akeem Olajuwon, they don't dominate the game in quite the same way that the big men of the past did.

It all began with George Mikan, a 6'10" giant who came out of DePaul University and helped make the Minneapolis Lakers the NBA's first great team. There weren't that many outstanding big men in the late 1940s and early 1950s. Mikan worked hard to become a great player, and he was able to lead his club to a number of league titles.

Shortly after Mikan retired, a quick and agile center came out of the University of San Francisco and began making an impact right from his first professional game. His name was Bill Russell. Rebounding and defense were his forte, and by playing to his strengths, the Boston Celtics were able to win 11 NBA championships in 13 years.

Russell's chief rival during the late 1950s and in the 1960s was a 7'1" giant out of Kansas. Wilt Chamberlain may have been the strongest man ever to play the game, as well as one of the most skilled. Wilt is the all-time leading rebounder in NBA history, and was its top scorer until Kareem came along. In fact, in just his third season in the league, 1961–62, Wilt scored 4,029 points for an incredible average of 50.4 points per game. He also once scored 100 points in a single game for Philadelphia against the New York Knicks. To say that Wilt could dominate a game is a gross understatement.

There were other fine big men back then, maybe a cut below Russell and Chamberlain, but outstanding nonetheless. Nate Thurmond and Jerry Lucas are two who come to mind. But back then almost all the good teams played off their center. He was what made the team go.

Russell retired after the 1968–69 season, a year before Abdul-Jabbar came in. Chamberlain played until 1972–73, when he still grabbed 1,526 rebounds for the Lakers at the age of thirty-six. And by that time Kareem was firmly established as the heir apparent, a man who could make a club a contender just by his very presence in the lineup.

In today's game the center doesn't have quite the same role. He isn't asked to get 20 rebounds a game, swat away key shots, score 30 points or more if his team needs it to win. Sure, a good team still has to have a good center, but the game no longer revolves around the man in the middle. That's why many long-time NBA observers feel Kareem was the last of the dominant centers. Yet Kareem himself won't claim that as a legacy. He prefers to say, "My legacy is that I played as well as I did for as long as I did."

Not even the man himself ever expected his career to last for two decades. After he had been with the Bucks for five years and had already won three of his six Most Valuable Player awards, someone asked him about his future.

"What I want to do is play 10 or 12 years in the NBA and see what I can do against the big guys. Then I'll go back to more normal things."

That never happened. Despite the lack of the dominant centers after Wilt left, Kareem stayed and helped the Los Angeles Lakers to five NBA championships. (He also won one with the Bucks.) When he finally announced that his twentieth season would be his last, the big guy had no regrets.

A youthful Kareem Abdul-Jabbar soars high as a member of the Milwaukee Bucks. Kareem led the Bucks to an NBA title in just his second season in the NBA. (Courtesy Milwaukee Bucks)

"It would have been wrong to leave earlier," he said, "and certainly I shouldn't stay any longer."

In spite of his huge record of success, basketball and life itself haven't always been easy for Kareem. It was Wilt Chamberlain who once said, "Nobody loves Goliath," as a way of explaining why fans often rooted against him. He was always the biggest, strongest guy—Goliath—and the natural tendency for fans is to root for the little guy, the underdog.

To prove the point, during his first few seasons in the league, the young Kareem often went up against the aging Chamberlain, using his speed and agility to score against Wilt. Very often the fans were vocal in their support of Chamberlain. He had become the underdog and Kareem Abdul-Jabbar was now Goliath.

Kareem was used to being the biggest kid on the block. It had been that way since he was a kid, a big kid. In fact, so many years have passed that there are probably people out there who don't remember that his name wasn't always Kareem Abdul-Jabbar.

He was born Ferdinand Lewis Alcindor in New York City on April 16, 1947. He weighed nearly 13 pounds when he was born, and all through his early years everyone called him Lewis or Lew. He was an only child and an intelligent youngster who had many friends, both black and white. But like all black youngsters, there was a point when he learned about prejudice. Some boys he thought were friends got angry one day and called him a nigger. It was something the sensitive youngster would never forget.

There was already basketball, though, and the court game would play a big part in young Lew's life from the time he was in the fourth grade. He was already 5'4" then, very tall for his age, so the other kids always wanted him on their side. But he hadn't played much, and really had to start from the beginning. His first real coach was a man named Farrell Hopkins, who coached Lew at St. Jude's School when Lew was in the fifth grade. He had the youngster lift weights for strength, and play and skip rope for quickness and agility.

By the time he was in the sixth grade he was already six feet tall, and he'd grow another six inches over the next two years. Farrell Hopkins continued working with him and also gave him some good advice.

"Because you're taller than everyone, people will always be watching you," the older man said. "So you have to be good. If you miss a lay-up, everyone will see it. And some people will laugh at you. Don't give them that chance."

Lew never forgot that. Nor did he forget what his father told him, to be proud of his height and always stand tall. He took that to heart too.

"People think I'm even taller than I am," he said, in later years. "They think I'm maybe seven-three or seven-four. That's because I stand tall."

By the time he was a sophomore at Power Memorial High School in New York City, Lew was already 6'10" and beginning to mature as a player. His coach at Power, Jack Donahue, said Lew had everything it takes to become a star.

"He could run and catch the ball," said Donahue. "That's very important for a big man. And he always had a great deal of pride. He didn't mind hard work and long hours of practice."

The work paid off. By his senior year he was a seven-footer and a super player who was coveted by nearly every major college in the country. He wound up leading Power to 78 wins in 79 games, scoring 2,967 points and grabbing 2,002 rebounds, both new New York City records.

Then everyone awaited the big decision. Where would Lew go? Some thought he would stay close to home and attend New York University or St. John's. But when he finally made his announcement, it surprised a lot of people. He decided to depart for sunny California and the University of California at Los Angeles.

When Lew entered UCLA in the fall of 1965, the varsity basketball team had just won two straight NCAA titles under veteran coach John Wooden. Lew had to play with the freshman team that year, but he and his first-year mates promptly went out and beat the varsity, 75–60, with the big guy getting 31 points. He seemed so good it was almost scary.

"Lew could play in the NBA right now," said Lakers' coach Fred Schaus, and others agreed.

His freshman team was unbeaten that year, with Lew averaging 33.1 points and 21.5 rebounds a game. The NCAA tournament was dubbed the "Last Chance Tournament" that year because everyone figured the next three years would belong to Alcindor and the Bruins.

They were right. From the time he scored 56 points in the first varsity game of his college career, Lew was the dominant player in the country. Coach Wooden said, "He was so good he frightened me," and Lew himself said he wasn't out to score points; rather, he wanted to play well and win ball games.

"Winning is more important to me than setting records," was the way he put it.

And win they did. The Bruins were unbeaten Lew's sophomore year, becoming national champs once again. The big guy averaged 29.7 points and 15.5 rebounds, and was named the consensus all-American along the way. In fact, the Bruins would only lose two games during Lew's three varsity years. One came against Houston when Alcindor was sub-par with an eye injury. The second was against a team that slowed the game to a crawl.

But in the tournament, the Bruins were always at their best. And as many had predicted, Lew led his club to three consecutive national championships. He was praised up and down by nearly everyone in the college game. He was already being called the greatest ever, ready for the pros, better than Wilt at the same stage of development. There was talk of raising the basket and making other rules to stop him. But Lew didn't feel the height of the hoop had anything to do with his game.

"It doesn't matter if you're seven foot or five-four," he said. "The whole challenge is to play well."

Oddly enough, there was a rule change before his junior year that is still referred to as the "Lew Alcindor Rule." The powers that be voted to outlaw the dunk shot, one of the most exciting plays in the game. Lew said it wouldn't hurt his own game, that he'd still get his points. But he felt it would hurt basketball as a whole. He turned out to be right. Soon after he graduated, the rule was repealed.

Lew also proved himself to be a hard-working player who was never completely satisfied with his game.

"People say there is no challenge left for me," he said after his sophomore year. "But I make my own challenges. My personal challenge is to improve my game and to keep winning."

Surrounded by fine players such as Mike Warren, Lucius Allen, Lynn Shackelford, and others, Alcindor and the Bruins dominated the college game for three years. The next question was where big Lew would wind up when he entered the NBA.

Though he admitted he'd love to play for the New York Knickerbockers, there was little chance of that happening. He wound up the first player chosen in the draft that year. The team that picked him was the Milwaukee Bucks, an expansionist club that had finished dead last in 1968–69. Though the New York Nets of the young American Basketball Association also chose him, Lew decided to go with the older league.

There was a lot of speculation about Lew's debut. It was against the Detroit Pistons, and he quickly showed he belonged by scoring 29 points, grabbing 12 rebounds, and blocking three shots in a full 48 minutes of action. More importantly, the Bucks won, 119–110, and it wasn't a fluke.

The addition of Lew made the Bucks winners. They wound up finishing the season just four games behind the Knicks in their division, with a 56–26 record. While the New Yorkers eliminated them in the playoffs, the Bucks and their talented young center were a team to be reckoned with.

Lew finished the season second in scoring to Jerry West, averaging 28.8 points a game. He was also third in rebounding with 1,190 boards, for a 14.5 average. His 337 assists were the best among the NBA centers, and he finished third in the MVP voting to the Knicks' Willis Reed and second to Reed in the All-Star voting.

Before the 1970–71 season got under way, there were two big changes on the Bucks. The first was the result of a trade that brought the great Oscar Robertson to the team. Now in the twilight of a great career, the 6′5″ Robertson was the kind of guard the team needed, a veteran to control the ball and direct the offense. There are still some today, in fact, who call the Big O the best all-around player in the history of the game.

The second change involved Lew himself. Though very few people knew it at the time, Lew had been studying the Islamic religion while at UCLA. By the time he was in the NBA, he had fully embraced his new religion, and with it took a new Islamic name. From this point on he was known as Kareem Abdul-Jabbar.

Because it was a time of black upheaval in the United States, some people felt that Kareem had become militant and antiwhite. He always denied that.

"There is no room in Islam for racial hatred," he said. "This is the way I feel in my heart. I cannot hate anybody. If racism messed up a lot of people who had to take it, then it must also mess up those who had to dish it out. I do not want to be that kind of narrow man."

Because he wasn't a naturally outgoing person, and never really felt at ease around the press or media, there were many people who didn't fully understand Kareem. It took years, until he was at the tail end of his career, for many to have some kind of understanding of him as a man and fully appreciate his greatness as a player.

He didn't play with the flare and rebounding tenacity of a Bill Russell, nor did he have the raw power of a Wilt Chamberlain. Yet in the minds of many, he did more things better than any center who ever played. He really began proving it his second year.

With Robertson giving the Bucks the floor leadership they lacked, the team really clicked. Kareem did everything asked of him in the middle, and the supporting players knew the roles. When the season ended, the Bucks had the best record in the NBA, finishing at 66–16. In fact, it was one of the best marks in league history.

As for Kareem, he was the league's leading scorer in his second season, averaging 31.7 points a game. On two separate occasions he had 53 points in a game, 48 in another, and 44 three times. He was also second in field-goal percentage and fourth in rebounds.

But even more importantly, he led the Bucks through the playoffs and to the championship. In the Western Conference finals, Milwaukee defeated the Lakers and Chamberlain in just five games, then smothered the Baltimore Bullets in four straight for the NBA crown. In just two years Kareem had shown the pros he was everything the collegiate people had said. He had made the transition without missing a beat. He had led an expansion team, in just its third year in the league, to a title. It takes a special player to do that.

Though the Bucks didn't win it again, it was no fault of Kareem's. He continued to show he was the premier center in the league, the logical successor to Russell and Chamberlain. The club was 63–19 the year after winning the title, but lost to the Lakers in the Western Conference finals in six games. Los Angeles had a 69–13 record during the regular season.

With Robertson showing his age and playing just one more season, the young Bucks were soon lacking a floor leader to handle the ball. Though they still were a winning team with Kareem in the middle, they weren't as good as an all-around team. Then, prior to the 1975–76 season, the big guy was traded to the Lakers. He wanted a change of scene, and since Chamberlain had retired, Los Angeles needed another center. It proved a great move for both Kareem and the Lakers.

Though the team didn't win right away, they were

always in contention with the big guy in the middle. Then, in 1979–80, the Lakers got a 6'9" point guard out of Michigan State, Earvin "Magic" Johnson, who turned pro after his sophomore year, when he led the Spartans to the NCAA championship. The Magic Man proved a great player right from his rookie year, and provided the glue that held the team together.

Continuing to center their attack around the now aging Kareem in the middle, the Lakers would go on to win five NBA titles in the 1980s and be the dominant team of the decade. And while he could no longer dominate game after game, Kareem could still turn it on. The proof came when he was named the Most Valuable Player in the playoffs in 1985 at the age of thirty-eight. He had also been the playoff MVP in 1971 when he was twenty-four. No other player in NBA history has stayed at the top of his game for so long a period of time.

In fact, Kareem averaged 23.4 points a game in 1985–86, when he was thirty-nine years of age. Though he began to show his age the next year, he was still a 17.5-point scorer at forty. The Lakers won yet another title that year, and they won it again in 1987–88, when he was forty-one and admittedly a shell of his former self as a player. Yet he still came up big when he had to in the playoffs, and it was widely acknowledged that despite his advancing age—ancient for an NBA pivotman—the Lakers would not have won without him.

He played one more year after that, seeing less and less time. It was finally obvious that the end had come. Yet the Lakers were still in the running for the title until injuries stopped them, guards Byron Scott and Magic both being hurt in the final against the Pistons.

As an aging star with the Lakers, Kareem could still hit his famed "sky hook," perhaps the most difficult shot to stop in the history of professional basketball. (AP/Wide World Photos)

By then Kareem had already announced his retirement, and in his last trip around the league, he was saluted and honored in every NBA city. Though he always had difficulty opening up to the media and fans, he smiled and joked often, and thanked the fans for their applause and appreciation.

He was a player who scored more than 38,000 points, the most in NBA history. He often did it with mechanical precision, throwing in his sky hook with nonchalance. Yet it was probably the most unstoppable shot, except for the dunk, in the history of the sport. Even his detractors will undoubtedly miss him.

The greatest player? It depends on the kind of player each person likes. Some might prefer a dynamic player like Magic, or the Big O, or Michael Jordan. Others might like a big man who does a few things dramatically well, such as Russell's defense and rebounding. Still others might prefer the explosiveness of a Julius "Doctor J" Erving.

But as an all-around presence for two decades, no one compares with Kareem Abdul-Jabbar. He was the man in the middle, perhaps the last of the great, dominant centers. But most of all, Kareem was a winner. He brought that quality with him from the first day to the last. And no one can argue with that.

6

WAYNE GRETZKY
The Greatest Ever

Sometimes it seems as if Wayne Gretzky has been around forever. The Los Angeles Kings hockey star, whose nickname is ''The Great One'' or ''The Great Gretzky,'' has been a record breaker and star for the entire decade of the 1980s. Yet at the outset of the 1989–90 season, he was not yet twenty-nine years old. That's because Wayne Gretzky became a pro at fifteen, joined the old World Hockey Association at seventeen and the National Hockey League a year later.

From that first season, when Wayne and the Edmonton Oilers came into the NHL after the WHA dissolved, the young winger has been a star. He scored 137 points in his first NFL season, getting 51 goals and a league-leading 86 assists. But that was just the beginning. By 1989–90, and still at the height of his career, Wayne Gretzky was already the all-time leading scorer in National Hockey League history.

Gretzky has been so completely dominant as a scorer that many people try to find a reason why he has obliterated all the scoring records. They will say the sport has changed, that there are too many teams, too many marginal players. They can't believe that The Great One has more skills than the greats of the past, guys like Rocket Richard, Gordie Howe, or Bobby Orr. But as more time passes, the facts can no longer be ignored. Wayne Gretzky may very well be the single greatest hockey player to ever lace on a pair of skates.

His accomplishments in a relatively short time are simply amazing. He tied Marcel Dionne for the most points in the league in 1979–80, then was the scoring champion for the next seven years in succession. He has also won the Hart Trophy as the Most Valuable Player in the league for an unprecedented eight straight seasons. In 1981–82 he became the first player in league history to score more than 200 points in a season, scoring 92 goals and passing for 120 assists for 212 points.

And to show it wasn't a fluke, he went on to score more than 200 points on three subsequent occasions, reaching a high of 215—on 52 goals and a record 163 assists—in 1985–86. But that's not all. Before a dramatic trade to the Los Angeles Kings in August 1989, Wayne had helped the Edmonton Oilers to four Stanley Cups during the decade of the 1980s. And in 1988–89 he helped transform his new team, the Kings, from a losing hockey club to one of the stronger teams in the league.

There's little doubt that Wayne Gretzky is something of a magician on skates. He may not be as fast as Bobby Hull, as strong as Gordie Howe, or quite as elusive as Bobby Orr. But he has a hockey sense second to none. It is said that no one can anticipate a play better than Wayne, or see what is happening all around him on the ice. That's why he makes so many brilliant passes for assists and so many great shots for scores.

Wayne Gretzky was born in Brantford, Ontario, Canada, on January 26, 1961. Like many other Canadian youngsters, Wayne learned to skate almost before he could walk. His father, Walter Gretzky, had once played junior hockey, though he never played as a professional. But he had his first son skating when he was just two years old.

Young Wayne took to the ice game quickly, and before long his father had built a rink in his own backyard. Wayne's mother was the one who worked the sprinkler to keep the ice smooth. So the making of a hockey player was a family affair. But that wasn't unusual in Canada. What was unusual was how quickly the youngster began to learn the game. Even though he was small and had to use a cut-down stick, he learned the individual skills—skating, shooting, passing —very quickly.

Because Wayne loved the game so much, he didn't mind the long hours of practice or the endless parade of shooting and skating drills set up by his father. He would practice each one until he could do it perfectly. And he would often skate until darkness fell, prompting his father to put up lights in the backyard.

When Wayne was just six he played in his first league, and while he scored just one goal, he was good enough playing against mostly older boys to make the all-star team. When he finished a game back then, he would go home and practice more on his backyard rink. It was a sure-fire formula for success.

As he got older, Wayne proved to be a fine all-around athlete. He ran track to build up the strength in his legs, played baseball to the point where the

Toronto Blue Jays once tried to sign him, and also played lacrosse, a rugged game involving many body checks.

"Lacrosse taught me how to roll a body check and how to spin away when a guy cross-checks you. This has carried over to hockey, and I think has kept me from taking too many solid hits and being decked."

By the time Wayne was eight years old he was beginning to attract a great deal of attention. It's not often that an eight-year-old is good enough to score 104 goals in a season. In fact, not too many hockey players of any age score that many goals.

Wayne was still small for his age when he turned eleven, standing just 4'4" tall and weighing around 70 pounds. Yet, incredibly, he went out on the ice with his team and scored 378 goals in 68 games. That's an average of slightly more than five and a half goals a game. No wonder he was on his way to becoming a national hero before he even reached his teenage years.

When Wayne was fourteen he decided to play Junior B hockey for the first time. He had to leave home and stay with some family friends in Toronto, which wasn't easy for a young boy. And he would be playing against boys fifteen, sixteen, and seventeen years old, a few even older. But that didn't stop Wayne. He continued to stand out.

In the mid-1970s Phil Esposito of the Boston Bruins was the top scorer in the National Hockey League. Esposito had set a record with 76 goals and 152 points in a season. One day Espo got a call from his father who told him he had just seen a kid who would someday break his scoring records. The kid was just fourteen and his name was Wayne Gretzky. His legend was already preceding him.

"Remember," Wayne's father once cautioned, "it's

going to be very hard for you to be normal and have a bad game. Every time you play a game, people will expect miracles.''

It turned out to be true. Wayne started feeling the pressure when he still lived at home in Brantford. That's why he welcomed the move to Toronto and into Junior B hockey.

''I wanted to move to a bigger city so I could have a normal life,'' he said.

But things would never be quite normal for Wayne Gretzky again. His second year in junior hockey he had 70 goals and 112 assists, and a year later he moved up to the Junior A level, playing for the Sault Sainte Marie Greyhounds. Junior A was one step below the pros, and Wayne was so good that he picked up the nickname ''The Great Gretzky'' for the first time. It also marked the first time that he was given uniform number 99, an unusual number for a hockey player, but one that Wayne was destined to make famous.

Then, as the 1979–80 season approached, the seventeen-year-old Gretzky began to feel as if he was ready for the pros. There were two leagues from which to choose then, the established National Hockey League and the fledgling World Hockey Association. Neither league normally took players as young as Wayne, but the Indianapolis Racers of the WHA said they wanted him.

Wayne and his agent decided to challenge the rule about seventeen-year-olds signing, and they won. Soon after, Wayne signed a seven-year pact for 1.75 million dollars. He was now a professional. No longer a little guy, Wayne was a six-footer and on his way to filling out to his present 175 pounds.

Oddly enough, after the battle to join Indianapolis,

Wayne Gretzky had plenty to smile about when he was with the Edmonton Oilers. He helped the Oilers win four Stanley Cups and had hockey fans everywhere calling him the greatest player ever to lace on a pair of skates. (Courtesy Edmonton Oilers)

Wayne played just eight games for the Racers. He scored three goals and picked up three assists, not startling stats, but good ones. Then, without warning, he was sold to the Edmonton Oilers, also of the WHA. It seems the Indianapolis team needed money and resorted to the old trick of selling a star player.

Wayne didn't mind. Edmonton was in his native Canada, and the Oilers indicated that they wanted him badly. In fact, as soon as Wayne began playing in Edmonton, he began to tear up the league. At age seventeen he was racking up goals and assists like a veteran superstar. So pleased were the Oilers that on January 26, 1979, Wayne's eighteenth birthday, they ripped up his original contract and gave him a long term, five-million-dollar deal that would make him an Oiler employee until 1999.

"Wayne Gretzky is the greatest young hockey player in the world," said Oiler owner, Peter Pocklington. "And one day he's likely to be the greatest older player."

When the season ended, Wayne had played better than anyone would have guessed. He was the WHA's Rookie of the Year and a second-team all-star selection. And he did it with 46 goals and 64 assists for 110 points. The 100-point mark had always been reserved for only the really great ones, and Wayne Gretzky had cracked it in his first professional season, which ended just a couple of months past his eighteenth birthday.

His boosters, like Peter Pocklington, said he was great already. But there were skeptics. Sure, Wayne was a talented young player. But he was playing in the WHA, a new league that was decidedly inferior to the National Hockey League. There was no way, his critics said, that Wayne would have scored 100 points in the NHL. Not at his young age, anyway.

That argument would soon be answered. The WHA just didn't have the finances to continue operation, and proposed a merger with the older NHL. The result was that several WHA teams, including the Oilers, would be absorbed into the NHL. So in 1979–80 Wayne and his teammates would be competing against the so-called big boys of the National Hockey League.

Expectations were high, and so was the pressure. But Wayne felt he could handle that.

"I've always had pressure," he said. "Every professional athlete is under some kind of pressure, and I just can't let myself think about it."

Weakened by a case of tonsillitis at the outset of the season, Wayne started slowly. Maybe he wasn't all he was supposed to be, some thought. But he broke the ice on November 1, when he scored a pair of goals in the opening period and later added an assist as the Oilers topped the New York Islanders, 7–5. At that time the Islanders were the best team in all of hockey. The game also signaled the emergence of Wayne Gretzky as a player to be reckoned with in the NHL.

From that point on Wayne was nearly unstoppable. He already had the great anticipation that allowed him to see what was developing on the ice. As he whisked around the rink almost effortlessly in his fluid skating style, he began picking up goals and assists as fast as anyone in the league. It wasn't long before the records began to fall.

In a late February game against the Washington Capitals, Wayne tied a 33-year-old record by collecting seven assists. His output that night gave him 96 points for the season, a new mark for a first-year player in the NHL. And a short time later, when he went over the 100-point mark, he became the youngest

National Hockey League player to ever achieve that milestone.

However, he wasn't through yet. On April 2 he netted his fiftieth goal of the year. It was another milestone because, once again, he was the youngest player to hit the half-century mark in goals. When the season ended he had 51 goals and 86 assists, giving him 137 points for the year, an incredible total for a kid barely nineteen years old and just in his second professional season.

In fact, he tied veteran Marcel Dionne of the L.A. Kings for the most points in the league, though Dionne was awarded the scoring title on the basis of more goals. Marcel had 53 goals and 84 assists for 137 points. Even though he wasn't awarded the scoring title, Wayne Gretzky still emerged the big winner.

He was given the Hart Trophy as the league's Most Valuable Player, and also took home the Lady Byng Trophy, given to the star who is considered the league's "most gentlemanly player." He had proved that what he had done in the WHA was no fluke. Playing in the stronger NHL, he was even better. In fact, many already felt he was close to the best.

Again, it was hard to figure exactly why. Some superstars simply have incredible physical strength and ability. But Wayne Gretzky, as talented as he was, had always been an intense student of the game. He was always watching, studying, memorizing the moves of the other players. As his coach at Edmonton, former longtime player Bryan Watson, said:

"Wayne is a lot like Bobby Orr and Gordie Howe in that he doesn't waste any energy running around the rink. I've seen him so many times go to a place, and then the puck comes there. Wayne is as fast with the puck as he is without it. And that's just tremendous ability.''

From that first NHL season the Gretzky legend continued to grow. As good as he was, he simply continued to get better and better. The next year he broke Bobby Orr's assist record of 102 when he notched 109 to go with 55 goals for 164 points, enabling him also to crack Phil Esposito's single-season scoring record. And, of course, he won another Hart Trophy. Then came 1981–82.

Years earlier, the legendary Maurice "Rocket" Richard of the Montreal Canadiens had set a record by scoring 50 goals in 50 games. The teams played just a 50-game schedule then, so Richard's achievement was considered nearly unreachable. Then, in 1980–81, Mike Bossy of the Islanders equaled Richard's feat by scoring 50 goals in his team's first 50 games. (They played 80 by then.) Still, no one was prepared for what Wayne Gretzky would do the following year.

The Great Gretzky simply went out and scored 50 goals in the Oilers' first 39 games! He achieved his milestone by scoring five goals in a single game against the Philadelphia Flyers.

"Never in my wildest imagination did I expect to score five times against a team like the Flyers," Wayne said afterward.

By the time the season ended, it was beginning to look as if Wayne could do anything he wanted in a hockey game. On February 17 his point total reached 165, enabling him to break his own record for points in a season. Eleven days later he bagged his eightieth goal, assuring him of at least a goal a game for the 80-game season. That was still another new record. In March he got the five hundredth point of his career, once again the youngest player by far to reach that milestone.

Then on March 25 he did what seemed the impossible, going over 200 points for the season. And when the regular campaign ended a short time later, Wayne was a record-setter again with 92 goals and 120 assists for 212 points. In just his third season he was all alone at the top of his sport. There were superstars, and then there was The Great Gretzky.

The only thing missing now was the Stanley Cup, the prize given to the winning team in the playoffs. The Oilers had built a strong team with some other fine players to support Wayne. In 1981–82 the club not only finished above .500 for the first time, but wound up with the second best record in the league behind the Islanders. In the playoffs, however, it was the Islanders who took their third straight Stanley Cup.

A year later the Isles made it four straight, but in the 1983–84 season the Oilers finally broke through. Wayne scored 205 points that year, adding 87 goals to his total. And he won the scoring title by 79 points over teammate Paul Coffey. But it was winning the Cup that made it all worthwhile.

Now Wayne really seemed to have it all. Not only was he the best player in hockey, but the Oilers were also the best team. At the age of twenty-three it almost seemed as if there were no more worlds to conquer. But the elusive center-ice man quickly proved that each new year presented a new challenge to him. And that challenge was simply to excel, improve, and win.

The Oilers took the Cup again in 1984–85, with Gretzky scoring 208 points with a record 135 assists. He also won the Conn Smythe Trophy as the Stanley

Cup MVP. Though the team didn't win it all the next year, the Great Gretzky continued to amaze. This time he scored "only" 52 goals, but he added an unheard of 163 assists for his career high of 215 points. The following season he scored 183 points, as the Oilers won their third Stanley Cup.

In 1987–88 the club did it again. Though they finished second to Calgary in the Smythe Division during the regular season, they rallied to take their fourth Stanley Cup. It was a strange year for Wayne. For the first time in eight years he failed to win the scoring championship. Limited to 64 games by injury, he scored 40 goals and 109 assists for 149 points, finishing second to young Mario Lemieux of Pittsburgh, who had 168.

But in the playoffs the great one had 12 goals and 31 assists for 43 points in 19 games, winning the Conn Smythe Trophy for the second time. All this, and he was still only twenty-seven years old.

That July Wayne was married in a lavish ceremony to actress Janet Jones, and the wedding sparked stories that Wayne wanted out of Edmonton. Because his wife was an actress and from California, he wanted to be traded to the Los Angeles Kings. But in truth, the rumblings had started even before that. Kings owner Bruce McNall had asked about Gretzky's availability, and the Oilers had indicated a deal was possible.

Finally, on August 9, 1988, one of the biggest trades in hockey history was completed. Wayne went to Los Angeles with two other players, Mike Krushelnyski and Marty McSorley, for center Jimmy Carson—the key man—and Martin Gelinas, first-round draft choices in 1989 and 1991, 1993 Entry Drafts, and cash. It was a huge deal, one of the biggest in sports history.

After joining the Los Angeles Kings, Gretzky (left) was still closely guarded wherever he went. Yet the Great One had already become hockey's all-time scoring leader before reaching the age of thirty. (AP/Wide World Photos)

Shortly after the deal was made, someone asked Kings' owner McNall if it was worth it.

"I compared the signing of Gretzky to the movie business," McNall said. "I said it would be like signing Clark Gable to a contract. And if we win the Stanley Cup, I believe we could write off all the expenditures we made to get Gretzky in one year's time."

As for Wayne, he was sad leaving Edmonton, though he supposedly could have vetoed the deal at the last minute, but didn't.

"I'm disappointed about having to leave Edmonton," Wayne said. "I truly admire all the Edmonton fans and respect everyone over the years. But there comes a time . . ."

Later he added, "The hard part was leaving the players. I miss the guys both on and off the ice. I can never replace those friendships, but I'll always have the memories."

There were rumors of hard feelings between Wayne and the Oilers' ownership, but the deal was done. And it wasn't long before the Gretzky magic really took Los Angeles by storm. The Kings had finished fourth in the Smythe Division in 1987–88, a losing team with a 30–42–8 record. They were eighteenth overall in the entire league, but with Wayne Gretzky in the lineup, the team became an instant winner.

Showing the ability to raise the level of play of those around him, Wayne had the club playing outstanding hockey. And the combination of The Great Gretzky and a winning team saw the attendance rise dramatically. The Kings finished with a 42–31–7 record in 1988–89. Their 91 points was the fourth-best total in the league, as they finished behind Calgary in the Smythe Division, but ahead of the Edmonton Oilers, who were third with 84 points.

As for Wayne, he did everything expected of him. Though he once again finished second to Mario Lemieux in scoring, he had a fine year with 54 goals and 114 assists for 168 points, a record tenth straight year he had topped the 100-point mark. While the Kings didn't win the Stanley Cup—Calgary won it—the franchise had the most successful year in its history. And much of the credit had to go to Number 99.

"Part of the problem in Los Angeles in the past was that there was no pressure on the hockey club to succeed," Wayne said. "A team has to have that sense that you win or else, and we have that now."

They continued to have it in 1989–90. By December the Kings were in a fight for the top spot in their division and Wayne Gretzky was once again the league's top scorer, leading archrival Lemieux and seemingly on the way to yet another 100-point season.

Armed with a huge contract that gives him lifetime security, Wayne Gretzky continues to work hard on and off the ice to improve his already great game. He has never been one to rest on his laurels. From the days when he practiced for hours on end on his backyard rink in Brantwood, Wayne has worked to be the best. There's really not much doubt now that he has reached that goal. Even the old-timers are admitting it. The Great Gretzky is the greatest. On the ice, he can simply do it all.

7

NOLAN RYAN
Strikeout Champion

It's almost like a story out of baseball's past. A raw-boned pitcher comes off a farm in a tiny Texas town, throws some old-fashioned hardball for a few years, then returns to the farm and the tiny Texas town he loves.

The key word, however, is *almost*. This story does have a few different twists. Yes, the rawboned young pitcher did come off a farm in a tiny Texas town. And, yes, he does plan to return to that town once his career ends. But in between, this old-fashioned country hardball pitcher has made baseball history. That's because his name is Nolan Ryan, the greatest power pitcher the game has ever known.

Want proof? In 1989 the 6′2″, 210-pound righthander from Alvin, Texas, was forty-two years old. It was his twenty-second year in the major leagues. Yet he was still firing his fastball in the mid-nineties and mixing it with a sharp-breaking curve and baffling change-up. The result was a 16–10 record for the Texas Rangers. But that wasn't all.

Nolan also led the majors with 301 strikeouts in just 239 innings of pitching. He was by far the oldest pitcher ever to fan more than 300 hitters in a season. It was also his sixth 300-plus strikeout season. And in his long, illustrious career, Nolan Ryan has struck out 5,076 big league batters. All of these strikeout totals are major league records. And to show again how effective he was, American League hitters could only bat a scant .187 against him.

Prior to 1987, in fact, Nolan already held more than 40 major league records, including an incredible five no-hitters. He flirted with a sixth on several occasions during the 1989 season and finally got it in June 1990. The only negative in his long career is his won-lost record. At the conclusion of the 1989 season it stood at 289–263. So while there is a good chance he will still enter the coveted 300-win circle, he had won just 26 more games than he'd lost.

But much of that can be attributed to luck, or the lack of it. No one will argue that the fireballing righthander pitched on weak ballclubs for a good part of his career. And while he was reluctant to talk about it in the early part of his career, as an elder statesman, Nolan is well aware of his situation.

"The most frustrating thing in my career was being on bad teams," he said in 1989. "I lost a lot of real close games. Under different circumstances, I would have been pitching to win them. That was frustrating."

Despite some outstanding seasons in the middle of his career, such as 1973 when he won 21 games and struck out a record 383 hitters, there were many people who still didn't consider Nolan one of the premier pitchers in the game. Sure, he was the fastest, but he was also wild and often lost about as many games as he won. It wasn't until later in his career that Nolan really began to get the respect he so rightly deserved.

The reason was simple. Most power pitchers, when they get into their middle and later thirties, begin to lose something off their fastball. To keep their effectiveness, they usually have to change their styles, begin using another pitch or two, depend more on guile and experience than raw power. But Nolan Ryan kept pumping his fastball and using his curve. And he kept striking out hitters, usually at the rate of more than one an inning.

In fact, at the age of forty in 1987, Nolan experienced something of a resurgence. He hadn't led the league in strikeouts since 1979, his final year with the California Angels before coming over to the Houston Astros. But in 1987 he whiffed 270 hitters in just 212 innings and led the National League with a 2.76 earned-run average. After that it was as if everyone had rediscovered Nolan Ryan.

"I can't give one reason as to why I've been able to do this for so long," Nolan has said. "I think mechanics and body type play a big role. I do know the older you get, the more important conditioning becomes."

Nolan has been surprisingly healthy for a pitcher who has thrown so many innings over the years. He's had surgery just once, when bone chips were removed from his elbow in 1975. Otherwise, except for a rib separation in 1978, his half dozen or so trips to the disabled list have been for various muscle pulls, usually in the legs.

But Nolan gets a good deal of his power from his legs and is constantly riding a stationary bicycle or "running" in the deep end of a pool. His legs are extremely important to him.

"I don't think I came to a conclusion one day that for me to be successful I was going to have to work extremely hard. Basically, that's been my approach to anything I've ever done. I never want to walk off the field feeling I got beat because the other guys are in better shape than I am."

The Ryan work ethic is something he picked up as a boy growing up in Alvin, Texas. He was actually born in nearby Refugio on January 31, 1947. But his family moved to Alvin a short time later. He remembers getting up early in the middle of the night to help his father deliver the Houston *Post*. That kind of extra effort in place of a laid-back, relaxed attitude became a normal way of life for him. Even at age forty-two it's his devotion to the work ethic that amazes those around him.

Rangers' pitching coach Tom House often meets Nolan for a workout at seven in the morning.

"I remember one day finding myself thinking," said House, "that we played a game the night before and here I was going down to meet Nolan at seven A.M. to lift weights. But once I got to know Nolan, I realized that's just the way he was. And that's also why he's still throwing as hard as he is at age forty-two. He does what it takes to prepare himself, no matter what that is."

For a while, though, it looked as if Nolan Ryan was just another flame thrower who couldn't put it all together. He liked sports from the beginning, and went through the Little League and Babe Ruth League programs in Alvin. At Alvin High School he was a baseball and basketball star, a thin, rawboned athlete with the ability to blow a baseball right past opposing hitters.

A number of major league teams were already interested in his strong right arm, but it was the New York Mets who grabbed him on the tenth round of the free agent draft in June 1965. The Mets were an expansion team, formed in 1962, and the organization was looking for good young pitchers. He was signed and sent to the Marion in the Appalachian League to finish out the 1965 season. And though his record was just 3–6 and his earned run average 4.38, he whiffed 115 batters in 78 innings. The Ryan strikeout legend was getting started.

It really took a giant step the next year, when he was pitching for Greenville in the Western Carolinas League. If his 17–2 record wasn't good enough, he also blew away hitters to the tune of 272 strikeouts in just 183 innings of work. And he was named Western Carolinas Pitcher of the Year. But he also led the league with 127 walks. So while the Mets knew they had lightning in a bottle, they also knew the young righty had to get his game under control.

He also threw two games at Williamsport in 1966, striking out 35 in 19 innings, then had a two-game cup of coffee with the Mets at the tail end of the season. He gave up five runs and five hits in three innings, but also fanned six. Nolan spent part of the next season in military service and the other part nursing a sore elbow, but when 1968 rolled around, the Mets kept him with the big club.

Though the team had been in last place nearly every year since it began, the ballclub was building around pitching. Righthander Tom Seaver was a rookie in 1967 and won 16 games. In 1968 the team brought up lefty Jerry Koosman, who would win 19 that year while Seaver was again a 16-game winner. The hope was that Nolan would mature quickly and join the other two to form a big three.

But it didn't happen. Nolan spent a month of the 1968 season on the disabled list with a blister problem on his pitching hand and was plagued by inconsistency the rest of the time. He wound up starting 18 games, compiling a 6–9 record and striking out 133 in 134 innings. He obviously wasn't as advanced as Seaver and Koosman.

Then came 1969, and Nolan pitched even less. Yet it was the year of the Miracle Mets, the team surprising the baseball world by going from ninth place in 1968 to first in 1969. Seaver won 25 games and emerged as a superstar, while Koosman took 17 after overcoming some early-season arm problems. Rookie Gary Gentry was the number-three starter and won 13 games.

As for Nolan, he shuttled between starting and relieving and only threw 89 innings all year. The ballclub just didn't have the confidence to give him the ball every four or five days and let him throw. He compiled a 6–3 record, a 3.54 ERA, 92 strikeouts, and 53 walks. But he pitched a strong seven innings to get a win in the playoffs against Atlanta, then saved the fourth game of the World Series with two and a third innings of one-hit pitching, finally fanning Paul Blair to end the game. A day later the Mets became world Champions.

"I don't think I realized how fortunate we were," Nolan would say years later. "As a young player, you just take for granted that those things happen so often."

Well, it would never happen to Nolan again. He would have to savor that World Championship as his only one. And when he returned to the Mets in 1970, he knew he wanted to start regularly, but wasn't sure the ballclub would give him the chance.

As it turned out, he would pitch two more seasons

in New York. He was used mostly as a starter, but was in and out of the rotation. And for a pitcher struggling to get his stuff under control, regular work is the best therapy. Nolan never had that luxury with the Mets.

He was 7–11 in 1970 and 10–14 in 1971. And both years he had fewer strikeouts than innings pitched. He was also wild, walking 97 in 132 innings in 1970 and 116 in 152 innings the next year. That seemed to be his biggest problem. Nolan continued to say he needed to pitch every fourth day like Seaver and Koosman. But for some reason the Mets refused to give him the ball on a regular basis. Something had to be done, and it finally happened in December 1971.

That's when Nolan learned he had been traded to the California Angels. Three minor league players were also included in the deal. The player coming to the Mets was former All-Star shortstop Jim Fregosi. The Mets wanted Fregosi to play third base. It turned out to be one of the most one-sided trades in baseball history.

While Fregosi was a player on the down slide, Nolan Ryan was a pitcher on the verge of greatness. The Angels wanted to find out in a hurry what Nolan really had. They gave him the ball every fourth day and let him pitch. It didn't take long for him to show exactly what he could do.

He started 39 times, completing 20 games. Nine of his starts resulted in shutouts and despite a 19–16 record—the Angels were not a good ballclub—his earned-run average was a sparkling 2.28. He also showed what his 100-mile-per-hour fastball could do over 284 innings, as he led the majors with 329 strikeouts. He also led with 157 walks, but it was obvious to all that he was a pitcher of enormous talent, a pitcher who had been held back by his treatment with the

A youthful-looking Nolan Ryan when he pitched for the California Angels. It was when he was with the Angels in the early 1970s that Ryan began breaking strikeout records. (Courtesy California Angels)

Mets. At the age of twenty-five he was finally getting his chance.

Then in 1973 he really began to cement his place in baseball history. Completing 26 of his 39 starts, Nolan became a 20-game winner for the first time, finishing with a 21–16 record and 2.87 earned run average. Along the way he became only the fifth pitcher in baseball history to throw two no-hitters in one season. He turned the trick against Kansas City on May 15, winning 3–0 and striking out 12. Then, two months later, on July 15, he blanked the Tigers, 6–0, again not giving up a hit, and striking out 17. When things were working right, he was simply overpowering, as overpowering as any pitcher who ever lived.

But the real big news came as the season wound down. Nolan was closing in on Sandy Koufax's single-season record of 382 strikeouts. It finally came down to one last start against the Twins, with Nolan needing 16 strikeouts to break the record. That was a large order to fill, even for Nolan Ryan. Sixteen-strikeout games don't occur every day. But Nolan was sharp that day, striking out one Minnesota player after another. It looked like he might make it.

Then he got a break. The game went into extra innings. In the eleventh the Angels got the go-ahead run. Trying to shut the door on the Twins, Nolan had 15 strikeouts to tie the record. Up stepped Rich Reese with two out. Nolan cranked up and fired his fastball. No frills. He nailed Reese to end the game and set a new strikeout record. Now no one could deny that Nolan had become perhaps the most dynamic pitcher in the game, a guy capable of throwing a no-hitter every time he took the mound.

He showed it was no accident the next year when he went 22–16 with another 367 strikeouts and a third no-hitter, a 4–0 whitewashing of the Twins. He had problems with bone chips in his elbow in 1975, but not before he threw a record-tying fourth no-hitter. But he came back the next two years to strike out 327 and 341 hitters, marking the fifth time in six years that he fanned more than 300 men. It was a remarkable achievement.

The problem was he still walked far too many hitters, and his won-lost records those two years were just 17–18 and 19–16. So despite his record-setting strikeout totals and four no-hitters, there were still some who said Nolan Ryan wasn't much more than a glorified .500 pitcher, a guy who lost almost as much as he won. It became even more frustrating for him in 1978 when he was on the disabled list twice—a hamstring pull and rib separation—and finished with a 10–13 record despite a league-leading 260 strikeouts in 235 innings.

But the walks, the lack of support, and the fact that he still didn't feel he had mastered the art of pitching, all bothered him.

"It hasn't been easy," he said. "But I guess it's all part of being Nolan Ryan. In fact, it may come that the day I retire I may feel I never got the complete control of my abilities that I would have liked to have. But if nothing else, I'll be one of the few guys to be successful in this game while being so wild. That's a novelty in itself."

Oddly enough, right after that down season of 1978, Nolan talked as if the end might not be far off, that his lifetime numbers didn't mean all that much to him.

"I don't have the love of the game to stay in it till I'm forty," he said. "I went into this game a hard thrower, and I'm gonna leave it like that. I'm not conscious of records . . . I don't really care about those things."

A year later, 1979, Nolan played out his option with the Angels. He must have felt he needed a change. After compiling a 16–14 record with 223 strikeouts and five shutouts, Nolan left to sign with the Houston Astros for the 1980 season. He had returned to the National League.

The Houston phase of Nolan's career was somewhat checkered. The Astros won their division in both 1980 and 1986, but were beaten in the playoffs first by the Phillies, then by the Mets. There were also some minor hurts. In 1983 he had two stints on the disabled list, and two more in 1984, this time for blisters and a pulled calf muscle. Then a hamstring pull on September 20 ended his season. In 1986 he was bothered by a sore elbow that limited the number of pitches he could throw. And again he was disabled twice by leg hurts.

He did throw a record fifth no-hitter in 1981, shutting out the Dodgers, and had an 11–5 record and league-leading 1.69 earned-run average in a season shortened by the players' strike. He won 16 in 1982, a year in which he fanned 245 hitters. He got career strikeout 3,000 in July 1980, then fanned batter 3,509 on April 27, 1983, enabling him to break the all-time record set by the great Walter Johnson.

For a while he and Phillies' lefthander Steve Carlton flip-flopped for the number-one spot. Then, on July 11, 1985, Nolan got strikeout number 4,000, still another milestone, and he upped it to 4,500 on September 9, 1987. By then Carlton had faded and the record belonged to Nolan. Now it was a matter of how high he could go.

Even during those somewhat mediocre seasons with the Astros in the mid-1980s, there was something about Nolan that was beginning to make baseball people take notice. Unlike other power pitchers, he didn't seem to be losing anything off his fastball. As he moved into his late thirties, he was throwing as hard as ever. And not just for one or two innings. Nolan could throw in the mid- to upper-nineties as long as he was in the game.

That's when he really began to get his due. And as Nolan himself had said, he was going to remain a power pitcher. He began working harder than ever to maintain his condition. When he regained the National League strikeout crown in 1987, fanning 270 batters in just 211 innings, he was already forty years old and suddenly looked upon as a geriatric wonder. No forty-year-old could throw like that. But Nolan Ryan was doing it.

Despite his increasing strikeout total, he was still dogged by bad luck. Even with the 270 whiffs and a league leading 2.76 earned-run average, he won just eight of 34 starts and had an 8–16 record for the year. He was 12–11 in 1988, adding his ninth strikeout crown with 228. Then he decided to become a free agent once more and signed with the Texas Rangers of the American League.

At the age of forty-two he not only became the Rangers' best pitcher, but once again perhaps the most exciting pitcher in all of baseball. By flirting with no-hitters on several occasions, he continually made national headlines. And when he continued to strike out more batters than any pitcher in the majors—more than Roger Clemens or Dwight Gooden or Mark Langston—he proved all over again what an amazing athlete he was.

And as he neared the magical 5,000 strikeout mark, Nolan reflected on what the number meant to him.

"I would like to achieve that because nobody has

Even past the age of forty, Nolan is still a fastball pitcher capable of racking up the K's. In 1989 the amazing, record-breaking righthander passed the 5,000 strikeout barrier and fanned more than 300 hitters for the season. (Courtesy Texas Rangers)

ever reached that number," he said. "It's like twenty wins in a season. It means a lot more for your reputation than nineteen victories. Five thousand is a number that sounds good."

It happened on August 22, 1989, at Arlington Stadium before some 42,869 fans. The Rangers were playing the powerful Oakland Athletics. In the fifth inning Nolan was facing Rickey Henderson, no less a superstar than himself. He cranked it up and fired a 96-mile-per-hour fastball past Henderson for strikeout number 5,000. But he didn't stop there. He fanned 13 A's that day en route to his 301 K's for the season.

By now nothing Nolan Ryan does should surprise anyone. After consulting with his wife and family, a yearly ritual, Nolan decided to return for the 1990 season. For a guy who said he didn't have the love of the game to play until he was forty, he's doing pretty good, going on forty-three and still throwing heat. He has outlasted all of his contemporaries. In fact, he has outlasted every fastball pitcher who ever lived.

And what of the day when Nolan Ryan finally decides to hang up his spikes? The Hall of Fame, once a question mark because of his won-lost record, now seems a sure shot. In fact, it's hard to see a pitcher coming along who will break some of his records, especially the strikeout mark. It would take just too long. That record will surely stand the test of time.

As for Nolan, he will return to his cattle ranch in Alvin, Texas, work the ranch, raise his family, and contribute to the community. There was never any doubt about that. Despite his notoriety, Nolan never had doubts about returning to his former lifestyle, proving once more that you can go home again, especially if you're Nolan Ryan, strikeout champion.

8

THE 1988 DODGERS

A True Miracle Team

In the eyes of many the 1988 Los Angeles Dodgers would be hard pressed to complete the season with a .500 record. After all, manager Tom Lasorda's ballclub had finished both the 1986 and 1987 seasons with identical 73–89 records. Not even close to .500. Yet the team surprised all the so-called experts, putting it together and winning the National League's Western Division with a 94–67 record.

Then came the playoffs. The Dodgers would have to face the New York Mets, considered the most talented team in the National League and maybe in all of baseball. How could the Dodgers hope to beat them in a seven-game series? It seemed almost impossible, especially since the Mets had won 10 of the 11 games the two teams played during the regular season. But again the Dodgers did the miraculous, winning the National League Championship in seven games.

Now it was on to the World Series. This time the Dodgers would be facing the Oakland A's, the best the American League had to offer. The A's had a power-laden team with the likes of José Canseco, Mark McGwire, Dave Henderson and Dave Parker. Once again the question was asked: How could the Dodgers possibly win? But this team of miracle makers proved unlikely champions. They won the first game with one of the most dramatic comebacks in World Series history, then went on to become World Champions in five games. And all the while people were saying it couldn't be done.

Was there a magic formula? You bet. It's called hard work, a total team effort coupled with some great individual performances, the same formula that has been winning pennants and World Series since the game began. But that didn't mean it was easy. In fact, maybe there was something of a miracle thrown in.

At the outset of the season Manager Lasorda was hoping to get strong starting pitching. But one of his starters, Tim Leary, was a veteran who had been with several teams and was just 3–11 in his first Dodgers season of 1987. Another was a rookie, Tim Belcher, who showed promise with a 4–2 mark at the tail end of 1987.

The two veterans expected to lead the staff were lefty Fernando Valenzuela and righthander Orel Hershiser. Valenzuela had been the mainstay of the Dodgers' staff since 1981, when he took the National League by storm as a twenty-one-year-old rookie. The native of Mexico had won 21 games in 1986, but was just 14–14 in 1987, and the Dodgers were somewhat worried about his arm. There were whispers that he had lost something off his fastball, perhaps the result of throwing too many screwballs over the years. Righty Hershiser was somewhat of an enigma in his own right. In 1985, his second full season with the ballclub, he had compiled a brilliant 19–3 record with an equally fine 2.03 earned run average. But he was only a .500 pitcher the following two seasons, finishing at 14–14 and 16–16 respectively. That's a lot of losses for a guy thought to have the potential to be one of the best in the National League.

The team seemed to have a solid bullpen, but they could only do so much if the starters faltered. So there was something of a question mark about the pitching when the season began.

Even when they were winning divisional titles in 1981, 1983, and 1985, the Dodgers weren't known for their heavy hitting. And the offense certainly hadn't gotten the job done in 1986 or 1987. But during the off-season of 1988, the team had signed a free agent they hoped would light a fire under everyone.

He was Kirk Gibson, the hard-hitting outfielder who had been playing for the Detroit Tigers since 1980. Gibson was a former all-American pass receiver at Michigan State as well as an all-American in baseball. He gave up the gridiron sport for the diamond, and was expected to become one of the game's premier power hitters.

But in his early years he was plagued by injuries, despite being a 6'3" 215-pound former football star who was used to taking a pounding. He finally emerged as a great clutch performer and leader in 1984, helping the Tigers win the World Series. He had 17 game-winning RBIs that year, was the MVP of the playoff series with a .417 average, and belted a pair of homers in the fifth game of the World Series.

Gibson's best season was 1985, when he had 29 homers and 97 RBIs, as well as 30 stolen bases. So he didn't have super numbers. But he was a no-nonsense

Longtime Dodgers manager Tommy Lasorda was
again the motivating force behind his team's success. The always optimistic skipper led his 1988
team to what most consider a miracle World Series
win. (Los Angeles Dodgers photo)

kind of player, a guy who would do anything to win. When he finished playing a game, his uniform was almost always dirty, and that's something the Dodgers lacked. Some said there was a country club atmosphere around Dodger Stadium. The team needed a leader.

They got their proof early in spring training. As the new kid on the block, Gibson was the butt end of a practical joke. Instead of laughing, he railed at his new teammates.

"I'm here to win baseball games, not play jokes," he said, and stormed out of camp. When he returned, everyone knew how serious he was, and slowly the other players got serious. Gibson's grit and determination soon began spreading to all of them.

The team had a number of solid ballplayers, but they would lose the power-hitting Pedro Guerrero to injury early in the season, then trade him away to St. Louis. That left Gibson and Mike Marshall to carry most of the power load, and like Gibson, Marshall often fell victim to injury. But the team could also count on second baseman Steve Sax, catcher Mike Scioscia, and center fielder John Shelby. Veteran utilityman Mickey Hatcher was another scrapper and hustler who could help light a fire under the offense.

After Valenzuela and the Dodgers were beaten by the Giants on opening day, Orel Hershiser took to the mound in the second game. He promptly threw a shutout. Because it simply evened the club's record at 1–1, no one realized at the time the full significance of Hershiser's whitewash. That would come later, during the final month of the season.

Hershiser would go on to win his first five decisions, helping to propel the team to a 13–6 start, putting them in the thick of the divisional race right

111

from the beginning. It was as if he had stepped forward, proclaiming himself the ace of the staff, the stopper, the guy who would get the job done in the tight spots.

Gibson, too, was proving himself worthy of the big contract he had received to come over to the Dodgers. His will to win and willingness to play hard every game had influenced his teammates. There was no laid-back atmosphere around the 1988 Dodgers. By May it was obvious they were a changed ballclub. Now the question was, did they have enough talent to win the division?

The Houston Astros were the team challenging Los Angeles for most of the season. The Astros did take a half game lead at the end of April, but the Dodgers quickly regained the top spot. They went up by as much as three games before the Astros cut it again and took the lead once more toward the end of May. The Dodgers had just a 22–15 record when the Astros retook the lead. The problem was that with the exception of Hershiser, the other starters were all around the .500 mark.

But when the Dodgers took the lead back on May 26, they were there to stay. Longtime ace Valenzuela had shoulder problems and would wind up disabled. But the club was still getting leadership and clutch hits from Gibson. Marshall was also having a solid year, as were Sax, Scioscia, Shelby, and Hatcher. Plus they began getting solid pitching from rookie Belcher and veteran Leary. Hershiser continued to be outstanding.

On August 24, Hershiser lost a tough 2–1 decision to the New York Mets, bringing his record to 17–8. The Dodgers had a 4½-game lead by then, and now the drama was really about to start. It began innocently enough on August 30, as Hershiser won number 18, beating Montreal, 4–2. In that game the Expos failed to score a run off the smooth righthander in the final four innings.

The next time out, Hershiser hurled a 3–0 shutout against Atlanta. Then he won his twentieth by blanking Cincinnati on September 10. That gave the Dodgers a five-game lead, and it was beginning to look like a divisional title was in the offing. In his next turn Hershiser was at it again. His third straight shutout was a 1–0 victory over Atlanta. And when he topped Houston, 1–0, his next time out, he had thrown 40 consecutive scoreless innings. The record was 58 straight goose-egg innings, held by former Dodger Don Drysdale. But it still seemed out of reach.

As the Dodgers continued their march to a title, Orel Hershiser continued his march to a record. Pitching against the Giants on September 23, he did it again. Shutout number five was a 3–0 victory. It raised the righty's record to 23–8 for the year and gave him 49 consecutive scoreless innings. It also gave the Dodgers an eight-game lead, and they seemed to have the divisional title wrapped up.

Then, on September 28, Orel took the hill at San Diego. Another shutout and he would tie Drysdale's record for scoreless innings. As it turned out, he didn't get a shutout and he didn't get a win, but he did get the record. The game was a scoreless tie after nine. Orel pitched through the tenth without allowing a run, giving him a new mark of 59 scoreless innings in a row. P.S.—the Dodgers won the game in the sixteenth.

When it ended, Tom Lasorda's ballclub had surprised all the experts and taken a divisional title. Hershiser led the way with his 23 wins, and had help

It was the brilliant pitching of Orel Hershiser that catapulted the Los Angeles Dodgers to the top in 1988. The veteran righthander finished the regular season with a record 59 straight scoreless innings and was a perfect 3–0 in the playoffs and World Series. (Los Angeles Dodgers photo)

from Leary with 17 and Belcher with 12. Jay Howell and Alejandro Peno led a strong bullpen.

Offensively, Gibson was the leader. He batted a solid .290 with 25 homers and 76 RBIs. He had missed a dozen games and played hurt much of the time. However, his efforts would earn him the National League's Most Valuable Player prize after the season.

Mike Marshall provided some power support with 20 homers and 82 RBIs, while John Shelby drove in 64 runs and Steve Sax 57. They were still not a super offensive team, but combined with the strong pitching, they got the job done. Yet despite all this, no one really thought the Dodgers would be a factor in the postseason. After all, the New York Mets and Oakland Athletics were the two acknowledged best teams in baseball. Most everyone fully expected a showdown between the fine Mets' pitchers and powerful Oakland hitters.

When the Mets took two of the first three playoff games, the Dodgers seemed to be in trouble. Lasorda had thrown his ace, Hershiser, in both the first and third games, and each time the righthander pitched well, but came away with a no-decision. Critics wondered how much the hardworking righthander could have left.

In the next two games, however, it was Kirk Gibson who provided the heroics. Despite his leg injuries, he belted a homer to win the fourth game and knot the series, then crashed a three-run shot in the fifth game, giving the surprising Dodgers a 3–2 lead in the playoff series. The so-called experts were beginning to bite their nails.

The Mets won the sixth game, 5–1, forcing a seventh and deciding contest. As he had in tough situations all year, manager Lasorda sent Orel Hershiser to the mound to face the Mets' Ron Darling. It turned out to be no contest. The Dodgers got a run in the first on a sacrifice fly by Gibson, then exploded for five in the second, sending Darling to the showers and giving Hershiser all he needed. The ace righthander pitched a five-hit shutout—yep, another one—and the underdog Dodgers were in the World Series.

But there was one major problem as L.A. prepared to face the free-swinging Oakland A's. Leftfielder Gibson was hurting and hurting badly. He had played the Mets series with a pulled left hamstring. But as usual, he played extra hard, not nursing the injury in the slightest. In doing so he also suffered a strained right knee. The Dodgers declared him out of the first game, maybe out of the entire series. That one was tough to believe.

Sure enough, when the opening lineups for Game One were announced, Kirk Gibson was nowhere to be found. In fact, he wasn't even on the bench. Rather, he was back in the trainer's room at Dodger Stadium taking treatments on both injured legs. Tough as he was, it just didn't look as if Gibson could play. Break number two for the A's was that Orel Hershiser wasn't ready to pitch. He had three starts and a relief appearance in the playoffs and needed at least another day of rest. Instead, rookie Belcher got the all-important first-game start.

The A's started their 21-game winner, Dave Stewart. Everything seemed in their favor. There was a temporary setback in the Dodger first when Mickey Hatcher belted a surprise two-run homer. But not to worry, the A's got it back with a bonus in the second. They loaded the bases off Belcher and, with two out, the powerful José Canseco blasted one over the center-field wall for just the fifteenth grand slam home run in

World Series history. And more importantly, the A's had come right back and taken a 4–2 lead. Was this the beginning of the onslaught?

Right after Canseco's slam, the television cameras scanned the quiet Dodger dugout, prompting announcer Vin Scully to comment, "And Gibson is definitely out of there."

Lasorda made a pitching change between innings, bringing in Tim Leary. Despite several Oakland threats, the veteran righthander shut the door on the hard-hitting American League champs. Meanwhile, the Dodgers got one back in the sixth, making it 4–3. Dodger relievers continued to stop the A's, but going into the bottom of the ninth, Oakland still clung to that one-run lead.

Oakland now had its ace reliever, Dennis Eckersley, on the hill, and he was the best closer in baseball in 1988 with 45 saves. Again announcer Scully told his audience, "The man the Dodgers need is Kirk Gibson, and he's not even in uniform."

But as the inning began, Gibson had set up a batting tee under the stands and was taking cuts, getting ready for one of the most dramatic moments in baseball history. However, Eckersley had gone to work and quickly retired Mike Scioscia and Jeff Hamilton. With two out, Mike Davis was coming up to pinch-hit for Alfredo Griffin. And that's when Gibson called Lasorda on the dugout phone.

"If you want me to hit after Mike, I can," he told his manager.

Lasorda told Gibson to get up to the dugout quickly. While that was happening, Davis worked Eckersley for a walk. And when the 56,000 fans at Dodger Stadium saw Kirk Gibson limp into the dugout and grab his bat, they erupted in a huge roar. But the

Dodgers slugger Kirk Gibson limped to the plate and hit one of the most dramatic home runs in World Series history to give the Dodgers the opening game of the 1988 fall classic. (Los Angeles Dodgers photo)

tough outfielder looked as if he was walking on eggs. That's how bad his legs were.

"I knew my appearance would really turn the fans on," Gibson said. "No question, they got my adrenaline going. And in that situation, you don't feel anything. I just knew I couldn't run."

But could he hit. At first it didn't look that way. He went after one pitch and looked clumsy and out of synch. But he also took a few, and suddenly the count was full at 3–2. Davis had stolen second, so the tying run was in scoring position. Gibson said he just wanted to make contact. Eckersley delivered and Gibson swung flat-footed, with no stride.

Yet he made solid contact, and the ball rose in the air toward the right-field stands. Would it go? The fans were on their feet and screaming as the ball carried into the seats for a game-winning, near-miracle home run!

It was hard to believe. Gibson limped around the bases in obvious pain. But he pumped his fist into the air again and again, a broad smile across his face. His shot had given the Dodgers an improbable victory and a 1–0 lead in the Series.

"I'm being paid to produce in the clutch," the hero said afteward. "That's what this is all about. I may look awful up there, but it can change fast. I am an impact player, and I felt it was my job and duty to the team. They had given me the opportunity by keeping the game close."

The one thing Kirk Gibson wasn't kidding about was his legs. They were in such bad shape that he would not make another appearance for the balance of the Series. But once would turn out to be quite enough.

The next day it was Orel Hershiser's turn. And Mr. Shutout was still on a roll. He blanked the powerful Athletics on just three hits to give his team a two-game lead. Now it looked as if the impossible might just happen after all. Oakland put the miracle on hold with a 2–1 victory in Game Three, but the Dodgers came back behind Belcher to win the fourth, 4–3. Now, in Game Five, Tom Lasorda decided to go back to his ace, hoping Hershiser had one more strong game in his right arm.

Oakland had Storm Davis on the mound, but by this time it didn't seem to matter to the Dodgers. In the first inning Franklin Stubbs singled and Mickey Hatcher hit his second home run of the series, giving the Dodgers a 2–0 lead. With Hershiser pitching, that could be all they would need. The A's got one back in the third, but in the fourth the Dodgers got another pair on a Mike Davis homer. It was now 4–1.

It became a 5–1 game in the sixth on a double by Rick Dempsey, and that was more than enough for Hershiser. Despite being tired, he continued to turn back the A's. In the dugout between innings he closed his eyes and seemed almost detached from the growing excitement around him. Later he admitted he was singing hymns to himself as a way to relax.

Though the A's got a second run in the eighth, the righthander closed them out, 5–2, making the Dodgers World Champions—World Champions who were not supposed to even be there.

But they did it the classic way, getting a solid team effort bolstered by several great individual performances. Hershiser was the series MVP, Gibson the emotional hero. Whatever they did, it worked.

Through the last month of the season and playoffs Orel Hershiser was almost unbelievable. In his last 14 outings he gave up just five earned runs in 101⅔ innings. That translates to a microscopic 0.44 earned-run average.

"I was a little worried in Game Five," Hershiser said when it was over. "I just didn't want it to be my one bad outing, a game that would have everyone saying maybe the rest of it was lucky."

No way. Perhaps it was co-hero Kirk Gibson who said it best: "As long as we all live, none of us will ever see any pitcher accomplish what Orel has done. It may be that no pitcher has ever stayed in a groove so long and so well. It's a measure of his great competitiveness and dedication."

Hershiser's competitiveness, Gibson's tenacity, and Lasorda's leadership. They got the bandwagon rolling, the rest of the team followed suit, and the result was a championship that was nothing short of miraculous.

9

MICHAEL JORDAN
Airborne Scoring Champion

Michael Jordan plays basketball much the same way the post office delivers overnight mail. He takes off quickly, flies high, and always reaches his destination. In fact, many now feel that the high-flying superstar of the Chicago Bulls has become the most exciting player in the game as the sport enters the 1990s. In truth, the man with the nickname of "Air" Jordan has been drawing the raves of fans, teammates, and opponents since his rookie year of 1984–85.

The sight of Michael Jordan flying through the air, mouth open and tongue out, has become a familiar one to NBA fans. Not only have they seen it on television, or during the annual league slam-dunk contest, but they have also seen Michael on posters, in magazines, and in commercials on television. The combination of his talent, quiet confidence and easy manner in public have made him one of the most visible athletes on the sports scene.

Like the other elite players of his time—among them "Magic" Johnson, Larry Bird, Patrick Ewing,

Akeem Olajuwon, Charles Barkley, and Carl Malone —it is ultimately his awesome talent that defines Michael Jordan. Though he was a two-time first-team all-American and twice *Sporting News* Player of the Year while at the University of North Carolina, the 6'6", 195-pound native of Brooklyn, a borough of New York City, has been even more successful as a pro.

He averaged 28.2 points a game as the league's Rookie of the Year, then was sidelined most of his second season with a broken foot. But he returned with a vengeance in 1986–87, winning the scoring title by averaging 37.1 points a game. He repeated the next year at 35.0, and again in 1988–89 at 32.5. But while his point totals might have decreased slightly, he was also doing more—playing defense, rebounding, passing, and even controlling the ball as he swung back and forth between guard and forward.

Needless to say, he has been an NBA All-Star, but he has worked equally as hard on defense and has made the All-Defensive team as well as being named Defensive Player of the Year in 1988, the same year he led the league in steals.

By now the picture should be clear. Michael Jordan is one terrific basketball player, a guy who puts a tremendous effort into each game he plays. He often takes a real pounding from bigger and stronger players, but keeps coming back for more if it will help his team win.

"I don't really feel the pain that much on a day-to-day basis," he has said. "But I do feel it after games, and there are times when I feel I've been in the league eight years instead of five."

He also admitted that the heavy workload every night has caused him to alter his style of play ever so slightly.

"I haven't been going to the hoop as much as I did in the past," he said toward the end of the 1988–89 season. "I've been shooting more from the outside to avoid some of the banging you get going to the basket."

Whereas there was a time in the NBA when the center, the big man, usually made most of the headlines, the all-purpose player is more often the man who makes the big news today. Instead of giants like George Mikan, Bill Russell, Wilt Chamberlain, and Kareem Abdul-Jabbar, it is Bird, Johnson, and now Jordan who are considered the pivotal players in the game. Despite a huge contract befitting his stature, as well as many attractive endorsement and commercial ventures, Air Jordan has continued to work hard and fly high. He looks at every game as a new challenge worthy of a hundred-percent effort. That's another reason so many call him the best.

Michael Jeffrey Jordan was born in Brooklyn on February 17, 1963. That year the top four NBA scorers were Wilt Chamberlain, Elgin Baylor, Oscar Robertson, and Bob Pettit, all future Hall of Famers. Bill Russell led the Boston Celtics to the NBA championship, while Celtic great Bob Cousy played his final season before retiring and another great, John Havlicek, contributed to the Boston effort as a rookie.

So there were plenty of great ballplayers around when Michael was growing up. He was the second of five children, all of whom were given positive values by their parents, James and Delores Jordan. The Jordan children were encouraged to work hard in school and be courteous to everyone they met. James Jordan put it this way: "We always tried to make something happen, rather than waiting around for it to happen."

Because he wanted a better life for his family, James Jordan moved everyone to Wilmington, North

Off the court, Michael Jordan is relaxed and friendly, one of the most well liked and popular athletes of his time. (AP/Wide World Photos)

Carolina, in the middle 1960s, and in 1967 was hired as a mechanic at General Electric's Wilmington plant, finally working his way up to a supervisor's position. Similarly, Delores Jordan began working as a teller at the United Carolina Bank and eventually became the head of customer relations.

Their values were passed down to all the children, and Michael has never forgotten what his parents gave him.

"I was lucky to have parents who cared," he said. "They gave me guidance and taught me to work hard."

Michael took to sports early. Baseball was his first love, but he soon began to play football and basketball as well. He even picked up his trademark of curling his tongue to the side of his mouth early on. It was a habit his father had when he did repairs around the house. Almost every picture of Air Jordan in midflight also shows the tongue coming out of the mouth.

By the time Michael reached D.C. Virgo Junior High, he was known as a fine all-around athlete, a three-sport star who still seemed to favor the baseball diamond. But his preference slowly changed, and by the time he got to Laney High School in Wilmington, it was the court game that held the most fascination for him. Like many basketball stars, his growth was sudden and fast. As a sophomore, he stood just 5′ 10″ and was far from a standout performer.

Because he was just an average player in a sport he was growing to love, Michael began practicing whenever he could. He even began cutting classes to spend more time dribbling and shooting. He was already the hardest-working player on the team, but by cutting classes, he eventually found himself suspended from school.

When Michael's father asked him what his goal was, the younger Jordan said he wanted to go to college. That's when his father told him he'd never make it by getting himself suspended from high school.

"I knew he was right," Michael said. "So I tried to change. I began concentrating more on my schoolwork. I knew I wanted to go to college and that I'd have to work hard to get there."

So he began to balance books and basketball. Yet he still didn't become a superstar overnight. It was a long haul. During his sophomore year at Laney High, he played jayvee ball and was extremely disappointed when a taller boy was moved up to the varsity for the state playoffs.

"I had averaged 27 or 28 points for the jayvees," he said, "and I thought I'd be called up. The coach let me on the bus because a student manager got sick, and to get into the game I had to carry the uniform of our star player. I didn't want that to happen again, so I worked even harder. And I grew."

By the time he was a junior, Michael had a routine that allowed him to practice with both the jayvee and varsity. So he was on the court from five-thirty to nine P.M., doing double duty in the drills, scrimmages, and wind sprints. Then on weekends he was back in the gym, looking for pickup games, practicing his skills, and paying his dues while many of his friends were out having fun. And by the time he was ready to play as a junior, he had grown from 5'10" to 6'3".

"It was almost as if Michael just willed himself taller," his father said.

Still adjusting to his increasing height, Michael averaged 25 points as a junior in his first varsity season. More importantly, he was becoming an impact player, a guy who wanted the ball when the game was on the line, and more often than not, came through with the key play. Perhaps the best example was in the title game of a holiday tournament that year. With the game close all the way, Michael scored his team's final 15 points, including the jumpshot at the buzzer that won the ballgame.

It was at that point that Dean Smith, the coach at North Carolina, first heard about Michael. Michael still didn't realize how good he was becoming. In fact, he said he couldn't imagine playing for a Division I school.

"It really shocked me when North Carolina started recruiting me," he said. "I never thought that could happen."

But it did. During the summer prior to his senior year, he was invited to attend the Five-Star Basketball Camp, which was a gathering of the finest players in the country. And for the first time Michael Jordan realized he could play with anybody. He simply excelled, leaping and soaring over the competition, playing defense and rebounding. He won nine trophies in two weeks and called it a "turning point" in his life.

Knowing what he wanted to do, and now having the confidence that he could do it, Michael signed to attend North Carolina early in his senior year. There would be no suspense, no recruiting war. He would be a Tar Heel. But even though his immediate future was set, he didn't let up. He still committed himself to excellence on the basketball court, to constant practice, long hours, and hard work.

As a high school senior he had grown to a height of 6'5", averaged 27.8 points and 12 rebounds a game. There were still many who had doubts that he could star at a school such as North Carolina. The Tar

Heels were usually among the best in the nation, and Coach Dean Smith stressed a controlled team game that often kept free-lancing individual talents under wraps.

Once practice began, Michael quickly realized that he could play with anyone. Apparently, Coach Smith agreed. Because when the 1981–82 season opened, the lanky freshman was in the starting lineup. And that, in itself, was an unusual move for Smith. Before the season ended, the confidence the coach showed in the freshman would pay huge dividends.

In his first game against Kansas, Michael had a modest 12 points in 31 minutes of action. But that was enough to give his confidence the boost it needed.

"After that first game I realized I was as good as anybody else," he said.

As the season progressed, both Michael and the Tar Heels continued to win and improve. By January they were the number-one-ranked team in the country and facing a showdown game with number-two Virginia, led by 7'4" center Ralph Sampson. In a hard-fought game, it was the Tar Heel balance that paid off. With players like James Worthy, Sam Perkins, and Matt Doherty to go along with the freshman Jordan, North Carolina won it, 65–60, to stay unbeaten. Michael had scored 16 points, hitting five of seven shots in the second half.

The team played at that same high level right through the end of the regular season. Then they raced through the NCAA playoffs right to the final game, meeting seven-foot Patrick Ewing and the Georgetown Hoyas for the national championship at the Louisiana Superdome. The Tar Heels had been to the final game on three other occasions under Dean Smith, but had never emerged the winner. Coach John Thompson's Hoyas would provide another stern test.

In the early going Patrick Ewing swatted away four North Carolina shots. Each was called goaltending since the ball was on a downward course. So the baskets counted, but the Tar Heels were now keenly aware of the big man in the middle. And for a time the pressing Georgetown defense gave the Heels trouble. The Hoyas led by as many as six points, but by the half the Tar Heels had cut the lead to one, 32–31.

The second half was a dogfight. The lead changed hands several times. North Carolina led by one, 61–60, when Georgetown's Sleepy Floyd hit a jumpshot with just 32 seconds left. That gave the Hoyas a one-point lead. Now the pressure was on North Carolina.

In the closing seconds it appeared as if the Tar Heels wanted to get the ball to James Worthy, who already had 28 points on the night. But as the offense developed, it was Michael Jordan, the freshman, who was on the receiving end of the pass. With 17 seconds left Michael had the ball on the baseline, leaped into the air and swished a jumper. The shot not only gave North Carolina the game, 63–62, but gave the Tar Heels the national championship as well.

Michael had averaged 13.5 points per game as a freshman, and had scored 16 in the title tilt, second only to Worthy's 28. He was also the biggest hero in the state, but it took a while for everything to sink in.

"It all happened so fast," he said, "that it just seemed like we had won another game and that was it. It didn't know how much it meant to people."

Despite his success and his heroics, Michael continued to work, and for the next two years was acknowledged as one of the best players in the country, an all-American with a bright future ahead of him in the pros. He had said he didn't want to be remembered for just one shot, but as a complete, all-around player. And it was obvious in both his sophomore and junior years that he was an improved ball player defensively, one who played both ends of the court equally well.

He led the team in scoring with a 20-point average as a sophomore, though the team wasn't as formidable as the year before, having lost Worthy to the pros. Then, in his junior year, he might have tried to do too much, tried too hard, for he experienced some strange scoring slumps early in the year.

"I was trying too hard to live up to people's expectations," he admitted later, "and putting too much pressure on myself to be as good as they had said I was. And I was paying too much attention to my statistics."

It wasn't long before he regained his all-American form. He played so well for the remainder of the year that some people were beginning to project him well into the future. One was a former NBA All-Star, Jeff Mullins.

Said Mullins: "The prevailing opinion always has been that Oscar Robertson and Jerry West are the two all-time best guards. But we may have to change that view because of Jordan."

The Tar Heels were 27–2 during the regular season of 1983–84, with Michael averaging close to 20 points a game once more. But they lost to a good Indiana team in the second round of the NCAA playoffs and didn't make it to the Final Four. Michael received his usual share of postseason honors, and still had one more year left. Or did he?

An increasing number of top college players were beginning to enter the NBA early. Former teammate

James Worthy had gone after his junior season and was an immediate success with the Los Angeles Lakers. Michael really had no more to prove as a collegian. After talking it over with his coach, his parents, and with Worthy, he decided to forego his senior season and enter the NBA draft.

"It wasn't solely a financial decision," Michael said. "It was also a chance to move up to a higher level and make a better life for myself."

Before joining the Chicago Bulls as their first draft choice, Michael played for Bobby Knight and the United States in the 1984 Olympic Games. He was one of the stars of the team, scoring 16 points in the gold medal victory over Brazil. True to form, he delivered in the clutch, scoring 14 of his points in the second half.

Playing for pay, Michael signed a seven-year, $6.15 million contract to begin his pro career with the Bulls. And as soon as he took the court as a rookie in 1984–85, the unanimous opinion was that he was worth every penny of it. Playing within the confines of Dean Smith's system at North Carolina, Michael was a 20-point scorer in each of his final two seasons. Yet in the faster pace of the NBA, it was quickly obvious that he had not yet tapped all the resources of his talents.

Playing against tough, seasoned veterans, the rookie was scoring at a pace nearly ten points better than he had in college, and was capable of great scoring explosions, as well as aerial shows unlike any since perhaps the heyday of Julius "Doctor J" Erving. Air Jordan was worth the price of admission, and with everything else, just his presence alone had made a mediocre ballclub competitive.

Once someone asked Michael about his incredible

On the court, "Air" Jordan is a spectacular player, an intense competitor who loves to fly to the hoop. Here, he goes in for two against the Knicks' great center, Patrick Ewing (33), as guard Mark Jackson (13) looks on. (AP/Wide World Photos)

midair moves as he went in for another of his electrifying slam dunks.

"I never practice the fancy stuff," he said. "If I thought about a move, I'd probably make a turnover. I just look at a situation in the air, adjust, create, and let instinct take over."

That instinct allowed him to average 28.2 points a game as a rookie. A broken bone in his left foot in just the third game of his second season put him on the shelf. He returned for the final 15 games, then in three playoff contests averaged 43.7 points, showing everyone that he was fully recovered from the injury.

The Bulls have slowly become a better team over the past few years. But in the eyes of many, the club still relies too much on its superstar. He is the best scorer in the game, the most exciting player, and the fans love to see him do his thing. But while Michael, like other fine athletes, is part entertainer, he is also a man who burns to win, and the ultimate is an NBA championship.

Charles Barkley, the 6'6" 250-pound forward of the Philadelphia 76ers knows what it's like to take a pounding. He is one who thinks the 6'6" 195-pound Jordan is being banged around too much.

"I've been in almost constant pain for three years now," Barkley said toward the end of the 1988–89 season. "I've got a bad back, bad knees, bad ankles, you name it. But I'll tell you the guy that the beating is going to affect more than anyone—Jordan. It will catch up to him someday."

Let's hope not. Michael Jordan is too much of a talent, too much of a champion, to have his career shortened by the pounding. He says, however, that he now has the ability to change his game, to fit in with whatever kind of team is around him.

"Individually, I don't think I have a thing left to prove to anyone," he has said. "All I'm interested in is winning."

The trick will be to find the right chemistry. The Bulls are a winning team. They just haven't yet taken the final step into the upper echelon of ball clubs. But they're close. Chicago's vice-president of basketball operations, Jerry Krause, has been trying to fit the pieces for several years. He says it isn't easy with a player as great as Michael Jordan.

"Michael is such a great competitor that he tends to dominate his own teammates in practice at times. And during games, his teammates often have a tendency to stand around and watch him. They sort of have that let-him-do-it attitude. It's hard not to be mesmerized by him."

A lot of people have been mesmerized by Michael Jordan since he exploded on the scene and won an NCAA championship with a great clutch shot as a college freshman. He made himself into that kind of ballplayer by long hours of hard work. And he hasn't stopped working since, a true champion in every sense of the word.

ABOUT THE AUTHOR

BILL GUTMAN has been an avid sports fan ever since he can remember. A freelance writer for eighteen years, he has done profiles and bios of many of today's sports heroes. Although Mr. Gutman likes all sports, he has written mostly about baseball and football. He is the author of Archway's *Sports Illustrated* series, *Baseball's Hot New Stars*, and *Great Sports Upsets*, available from Archway Paperbacks. Currently, he lives in Poughquag, New York, with his wife, two stepchildren, and a variety of pets.